WEAVING THE CARPET OF LIFE

"The Sacred Feminine Power"

"Noons"

The 3 White Women

VIE Loriot de Rouvray

ISBN: 979-8-9905885-5-4 PB
ISBN: 979-8-9905885-6-1 HB

"Nowadays, no one wants to hear the truth. The truth hurts, troubles, upsets, and all is made in society to cover up the truth."

"Whistleblowers and Awakened people are always taken for lunatics or conspirators, but in the end, they are always proven right."

"One day you will come to understand that those you ridiculed and qualified as conspirators were in reality your family, loving you enough to tell you the truth."

God said, "Let there be Light; and there was light. And God saw the light, that it was good: and God divided the light from the darkness." Genesis 1:3-13

CORE-SOURCE-DIAMOND

I want to thank the Group of the Star Chamber:

- Chanceliere Eloise Duvet
- Ronald Cole
- Asuba
- Sun King Louis XIV
- Zolima
- Tkeswanna

NOTE FOR READERS

Each of my books is a different and unique experience that will reshape your understanding of reality, spirituality, and the Self. It takes you on a spiritual journey for your growth and well-being, which are powerful steps to personal growth and self-transformation. They should be read in chronological sequence.

These books are written quite differently; they are intended to bring a new understanding of reality to humankind. It will allow humankind to evolve much more quickly. It's encoded in the books to open up the consciousness.

The readers of these books act as a bridge between the mystical realm in the path of human awakenings. It will change the way you interact with other people and will make you understand your motivation.

- 9.1.1. Complete Guide To Natural Healing (Book 1) (This book was guided by the Archangel Michael)
- 9..1.1. Aroma Essential Therapy (Book 2)

"The book series "Expansion of Mind and Consciousness"

- Destiny of the Dog; Beware of the Almighty (volume 1)
- Time is Ticking; The Fifth Amendment (volume 2)
- Karma Through The Window of Time (Volume 3)
- New Century, New Era, New Experiences (volume 4)
- Intonex (volume 5)
- The Genome of The Ancient Creators "ABBA EBEN" (volume 6)
- The Phoenix with the Chrystal Plumage (volume 7)
- The Great Awakening; Remembering the Sacred Music (volume 8)
- Weaving The Carpet of Life; The Sacred Feminine Power" (volume 9)

TABLE OF CONTENTS

INTRODUCTION

What I am bringing forth is from a higher source, and there is information attached to the written words, but people don't hear it. The book and the energy associated with the information are very powerful. It is spiritual and sacred, Mary's feminine transmission encoded with vibrational healing. Reading it is a soul recalibration.

In some interpretations, weaving the carpet of life is seen as a symbol of ascent and transcendence. It represents the journey towards higher states of consciousness or enlightenment. Bridging Worlds: The weaving carpet can also be seen as a bridge between the earth and the divine realms.

Noons is a subtle, barely perceptible bit of energy directed at the three Marys.

In biblical timekeeping, the ninth hour roughly corresponds to 3:00 p.m. on a modern 12-hour clock. It is the ninth hour for the 3 white women to weave the carpet of Life. Could it be the three Marys? And if it was the ninth hour for the 3 white women weaving the carpet of life? Could Mary Jacob and Mary Salome join Marie-Madeleine to end the battle to win against Agenda 2030?

Mary Magdalene, or Marie Madeleine, Jesus' wife, was one of the women who traveled with Jesus and helped support his ministry "out of their resources".

Mary of Cleopas, Sister of Mother Mary and Mary Salome, mother of James and John's disciples, wife of Zebedee. Mary Salome traveled with San Sarah, her maid, and part of the group who landed near Sainte Maries- de- la- Mer Provence, after a voyage from the Holy Land. Saint Sarah, also known as San Sarah, is the Patron Saint of the Romani people. The center of her veneration is Sainte Marie de la Mer, a place of pilgrimage for Romani in the Camargue, in Southern France.

The Three Marys carry personal attributes or iconic accessories. They symbolize Faith, Hope, and Love. The theological virtues are present in the Easter mystery of God.

- Mary Clopas (sometimes alternated with Mary Jacob) – holding a broom
- Mary Salome – holding a thurible or censer
- Mary Magdalene – holding an alabaster chalice or jar.

The three Marys symbolize, respectively, faith, hope, and love. The theological virtues are present in the Easter mystery. God, in His providence, brought each of these Marys to the cross that fateful day. And in His loving mercy, He made each of the three Marys a witness of the Risen Christ. Mary Magdalene is a witness to the crucifixion of Jesus and is also present at his burial, as the first to witness Jesus's resurrection.

Time for the 3 white women to come back to end Agenda 2030. With the corrupt United Nations socialists' globalist policies being rolled out by the corrupt Government system, and useless and corrupt local councils. They are called to unveil the hidden truth.

To help End smoke genes the spread of bacteria, cancer, and HIV while they are committing millions of the most horrifying crimes in our world history. Help people in need, community service, literacy, education...

The rights of citizens are to be protected, whether these rights are listed or not. This means rights are not specifically listed in the Constitution, and examples include the right to privacy, the right to travel, and the right to make decisions about one's body.

All the rights not listed in the Constitution belong to the people, not the Government.

The corrupt and self-elected government will try to keep its grip on power by projecting a false image of the Anunnaki returning. They will try to manipulate the brains of humans to admit to their return, a false image of who they are, and keep power. But they cannot do anything without disclosing first, so they made a movie... It is a story about power, control, and manipulation.

SYNOPSIS

VIE continues to have powerful dreams, visions, and visitations and is helped by entities from other realms and aliens. Physical Reality comes from Dreams, Visions and Imaginations and Quantum is incorruptible.

She and her blue flame now embark on a new, thrilling adventure to live with other people in another realm. King Louis the XIV has joined to help VIE and the God Duo Earth Mission. When she astral travels and meets them, she receives crucial information and answers from star sisters, or spiritual people from different realms.

Big changes are coming. The world's lakes, oceans, rivers, and waterways will be restored to purity, as will soil and farmland. Using toxic chemicals on food will cease, and pharmaceutical companies will be dismantled. Holistic practices will take over and will be the norm. Governments will be eradicated, and the people of each nation will govern themselves. Clean energy will be utilized. Hospitals will be equipped with new alternative and holistic technologies, like med-beds and therapies, and treatments. The essence of the Divine Feminine is still present, waiting to be acknowledged.

This odyssey began when VIE met CHADD in a wheelchair and felt a deep and strong connection, inexplicable. She got to know him better and became enveloped in a world of mysticism, government conspiracies, religions/cults, and upcoming prophesied events. They entered a world of lies deception, hope, and pain. Her spiritual journey began when she joined forces with her blue flame, CHADD, to bring the words of Jesus.

Henri was a professor who lived near an Indian tribal reservation and had a son, Edward, with his wife, Martha. Edward married Ethel, and they had a son, CHADD, who was diagnosed with several behaviors and mental problems after his dad took him to the government hospital that his father, Edward, used at the request of the NSA. At the age of five, they started to do testing on CHADD to understand his unique ability. Though he was never sick, CHADD was given multiple drugs at the age of five. Then Edward divorced, and during Edward and Ethel's separation, he started dating a coworker named Katherine, an archon known as the harsh woman, or surnamed the Surrogate, working hand in hand with CHADD's half-brother, Paul. Katherine's son was a sworn law enforcement officer when that was taking place. Paul, the mafioso Carlos, and Katherine were all involved with the corrupt government. The government would take the drugs from the drug dealers in the West, send them to Miami for sale in Florida, and generate money for the government's clandestine operations.

CHADD spent time in hospitals and medical centers, and during his stay in the hospital, a group called Guardians revealed themselves. They were the Cathari. There were two elements to them, the Perfecti and the Believers. The Perfecti were helpful and wanted to bring people closer to God. They defeated Hitler. The Believers were the Nazis and are the serial killers of today and the many world leaders who destroyed rather than created. Extremely intelligent and hypnotizing at the same time, some of the Believers had guidance in genetic reproduction thousands of years ago, before and after the great flood, to create creatures seen throughout history as vampires, werewolves, Bigfoot, and reptilians.

CHADD is a baker's act, a drugged-up ward of the state, holds the keys to the Divine wisdom, and with VIE brings humanity into the light of God just when it all seems lost. But all of this was a treat to the Anunnaki, who wanted the Earth for themselves. So they manipulated the story of Christ to be successful with the takeover of Earth...A never-ending battle of good and evil: the modern world is a literal and figurative warzone.

The straightest path to the truth is to expose all information that is officially forbidden.

The secret Government controls the population through false information. Christ was a healer; He worked with the emotional body, and He resurrected from the dead. The Church stripped away the virility of Christ by hiding His true relationship with Marie-Madeleine, and the male was emasculated and the female denied.

The Illuminati are in key places, and all institutions are corrupted. Their agenda is to reduce the population and to manipulate humanity by keeping them under their control through drugs, flu, antibiotic shots, implanted diseases, weather catastrophes, and endless wars, and division of the population.

The Thuggees' medical doctors from India reincarnated and infiltrated every hospital in the state. They keep CHADD by court orders, in drugs, and in a foggy state between Mental Hospitals and asylums. They shot him with dangerous drugs, brainwashed, programmed then manipulated him, in the land of freedom.... They sent an Asian couple to steal the Vajra from VIE after putting some drugs in her drink. She has been poisoned more than once, they invaded her body with alien parasites, crippled her hands and her feet, attacked first her knees and finally, her legs and much more. They were planning to kill her by targeting her heart.

Jesus and Mary-Madeleine are returning to demonstrate the path of Oneness and Divine Love. To awaken new frequencies within one's being, defragment old programming that no longer serves so that humanity can embrace the Light and Sound of creation and expand consciousness.

Christ delivered His bloodline and star codes through the Goddess (Marie-Madeleine), bringing the ultimate creativity that could transmute human violence: "The Eucharist," true Christ.

There is a powerful message brought to the world, and it is about the Matrix and the Ascension process to reach the Golden Age, with warnings and future predictions that you may or may not want to hear but have to hear.

Once you remember your multidimensionality, then Christ will awaken in you. And it is Time! The Golden Age is within reach.

CHADD & VIE have the knowledge that can be used to enlighten your world and help resolve the difference that separates you on Earth.

"Henri the Professor, who is CHADD's grandfather, has now passed away from Alzheimer's after being found lost in a hospital hallway from a heart attack. Edward, CHADD's father, died after a long battle against diabetes II. Katherine now has very advanced diabetes II after eating a bad diet, her son Paul has cancer, and her nephew hacks computers for a living for the cabal. The three hybrids don't have much time left to live on Earth as they have found a way to separate CHADD and VIE." Temporarily!

While CHADD is kept on drugs, VIE is helped and guided by entities from other realms and Aliens. It's about an illegal program to experiment with mind control initiated by the CIA, and how the moon influences life on Earth. The UN thought to eliminate all borders and genders to create an atheist human field human race since they realized that Christianity was based on the Essene teaching. The Roman Empire stepped in to eliminate the teachings from the Essene, the human ascension: the transformation of your body into a body of light or the rainbow body.

Other civilizations are back here to help the earth, just when the CIA & NSA target anyone, anywhere, anytime on Earth with mind control technology and program their victims, entraining the brain to their remote neural monitoring system while blaming the population for Global warming that they create.

Be Careful, there is no ascension without Spirituality or Divine Reconnection, and when you awaken and become a serious co-creator, the cabal will have no more power to rule the world. But you have to make it. Watch out for Gurus, false prophets, and cults, and the Bible has been altered.

Christ will come down from revolving Light clouds with a multitude of Masters gathered around him. Many will be glad and many will be sorrowful at the sight, for they did not recognize that their Masters were in the midst, walking among the Earth. It is the ability to enrich the world through the journey of the mystics, the universal voyage. Each individual has to travel in their own time for it reveals the path of knowing and transcends time and space.

This path reveals the higher truth of personal evolution, which you are invited to find.

The teaching of Jesus Christ is essential to the awakening happening now. It is teaching entirely based on love and respect for each other. Non-believers in God are used for mind control or real demonic possession. The fallen angels, the Illuminati, have abused the physical creations. The archons are inorganic and artificial and make a bad copy of our original reality. The Illuminati want a one-world government, and they selected electronics to be brought to Planet Earth for that and to keep control of humans. The pineal gland is the key to ascension and the higher vibration, and the cabal does not want you to regenerate it.

Once the regeneration process begins, they won't be able to stop it. (There is no need for a children 's blood transfusion.) People will no longer be susceptible to controlling human beings on the planet. What if the Library of Alexandria was the link to today's affliction of the world and the Cabal? The Templars fought the forces of Islam in Spain and on the sunbaked hills where Jesus lived and died. The knowledge that the Cabal has in sacred geometry forms to control and create a single government. But the new template is here, the New Tools for the New Earth.

The falling away of power and the manipulation that is taking place stimulate life forms to evolve into something better. So there is a great benefit in this whole process, and nothing to be frightened of, absolutely nothing. There is absolutely nothing to fear in these coming times. As you begin to honor yourself, you will draw to yourself opportunities beyond your conception.

The essence of the Divine feminine is the source of creative realization linked to the heart center. The most powerful magnetic energy. It represents a sacred life-giving energy that transcends gender binaries.

We are living in a world that tells women to be powerful, then punishes them for it. Women are expected to show up, speak up, work hard, take charge, but to not make anyone uncomfortable while they do it.

Now is the time when males and females are equal. When these two energies are in balance, it will make a perfect being like Christ.

PROLOGUE

In this groundbreaking new book of the series, VIE reveals what has been lost in our modern world and explains the multidimensional nature that drives the evolution of consciousness, providing a journey through complex ideas of modern science and esoteric wisdom.

The Ninth Wave Quantum, although achieving this is an individual process, is ultimately about manifesting a collective and consistent goal originating with the Divine. The inner realignment. Enlightened individuals have arrived at a place where the quantum state of the ninth world dominates their point of view on life. The largest and most to learn. It is when the Alchemy of the Ninth activates the full spectrum of consciousness. Big changes are coming

This visionary, new, and innovative adventure began when VIE met CHADD in a wheelchair and felt a deep and strong connection, inexplicable. She got to know him better and became enveloped in a world of mysticism, government conspiracies, religions/cults, and upcoming prophesied events. They entered a world of lies, deception, hope, and pain. Her spiritual journey began when she joined forces with her blue flame, CHADD, to bring the words of Jesus.

Henri was a professor who lived near an Indian tribal reservation and had a son, Edward, with his wife, Martha. Edward married Ethel, and they had a son, CHADD, who was diagnosed with several behaviors and mental problems after his dad took him to the government hospital that his father, Edward, used at the request of the NSA. At the age of five, they started to do testing on CHADD to understand his unique ability. Though he was never sick, CHADD was given multiple drugs at the age of five. Then Edward divorced, and during the time of Edward and Ethel's separation, he started dating a coworker named Katherine, an archon known as the harsh woman, or surnamed the Surrogate, working hand in hand with CHADD's half-brother, Paul. Katherine's son, Paul, was a sworn law enforcement officer at that time. Paul, Carlos, and Katherine were all involved with the corrupt government. The government would take the drugs from the drug dealers in the West, send them to Miami for sale in Florida, and generate money for the government's clandestine operations.

CHADD spent time in hospitals and medical centers, and during his stay in the hospital, a group called Guardians revealed themselves. They were the Cathari. There were two elements to them, the

Perfecti and the Believers. The Perfecti were helpful and wanted to bring people closer to God. They defeated Hitler. The Believers were the Nazis and are the serial killers of today and the many world leaders who destroyed rather than created. Extremely intelligent and hypnotizing at the same time, some of the Believers had guidance in genetic reproduction thousands of years ago, before and after the great flood, to create creatures seen throughout history as vampires, werewolves, Bigfoot, and reptilians.

CHADD is a baker's act, a drugged-up ward of the state, holds the keys to the Divine wisdom, and with VIE brings humanity into the light of God just when it all seems lost. But all of this was a treat to the Anunnaki, who wanted the Earth for themselves. So, they manipulated the story of Christ to be successful with the takeover of Earth...A never-ending battle of good and evil: the modern world is a literal and figurative warzone.

The victory for the First Amendment is not over; allies like Germany and Italy are cracking down on free speech in completely draconian ways, arresting people for daring to state opinions their government does not like.

The current dark and greedy leaders will no longer hold their positions everything will begin to fall apart like a domino effect.

Mary's truths will be revealed to awaken the rest of the people with the sacred feminine Archetype. The feminine essence is linked to the heart center. It is the most powerful magnetic energy source.

The Divine feminine energy is a spiritual and interconnectedness of all life.

CHAPTER 1
The Essence Of The Divine Feminine

Floating down from the cloud, I witnessed the time of troubles, basically the world Karma coming to that point where it is transducing a whole new energy. It immediately reminded me of Atlantis. Apparently, we were CHADD, and I further back in time in my actual vision.

The storm is here. Quantum Monetary System (QFS) is destined to destroy Lucifer's money. The pyramid is upside down. The curtain is turned off. The energy will not be used negatively anymore.

The truth can no longer be hidden. The veil has been torn off the most sacred deception on Earth. Expose a system of spiritual blackmail, money laundering, and trafficking of elite hidden behind altars and incense. Faith was a lie, is just a cover. Faith was a lie; it was a front. The Vatican is not just the guardian of spirits. It is a vault of the shadow state, trillions of money flowing through bloody hands, secret charities, fraudulent investments, and secret channels of gold trading. But the era is ending. The world is watching the expulsion of demons from the empire that once ruled heaven and earth.

When we tried to change the DNA and bring forth a more feminine energy back in the days of Atlantis and it failed. We were expert scientists working together in a lab, and we were killed. We both know what the reason is.

The reason it failed was that the energy was used in a negative way by the beings in Atlantis. It would have raised and caused the union between the Divine male and the divine female. What the dark forces already did not want at that time.

Therefore, the planet Earth went through many, many thousands of years with women being subjugated and the feminine energy being suppressed.

There is a meeting of the council, and they are discussing all types of things. There must be decisions for ... it concerns lower vibrations, and those that haven't reached the higher planes or higher vibrations, and the essence of the Divine Feminine.

It seems like for each lower vibration, there are certain things they need to learn to be able to elevate their vibrations to a different plane. The council helps them to make the decisions.

The essence of the Divine Feminine never truly vanished. It is still present, waiting for you to acknowledge, embrace, and bring it back into the balance of our lives and the world.

The Divine Feminine is a concept encompassing various attributes related to the feminine energy. It's primarily associated with characteristics such as intuition, community, empathy, and collaboration across different cultures and religions. Goddesses have been revered as representations of the Divine Feminine, each emphasizing specific aspects of this profound concept.

But understanding the Divine Feminine goes beyond just recognizing these characteristics. It is about appreciating and incorporating them into yourselves and your lives. By doing so, and by achieving a balance with your masculine energies, it can lead to a more enriched and harmonious existence.

The Divine Feminine represents a sacred, life-giving energy that transcends gender binaries. It is a force of creation, nurturing, and intuition, a wellspring of wisdom and compassion that has been celebrated across cultures and belief systems throughout human history.

The woman, the eternal feminine, is a sunderable principle from the eternal Masculine principle.

But now is the time when both are equal. The male and the female divine energies will join, and it will make a perfect being like Christ, when these energies are in balance. These energies have been out of balance for thousands of years, and it has caused many problems on the planet.

When the DNA structures are altered, the divine energies can unite. The male-female, the Yin and Yang, of the God energies can unite, and perfection will be upon the planet. As the perfection within the bodies.

The divine energies have not been balanced within the psyche or even within the physical mind, but the psyche that comes with it, the body manifests. They were out of alignment and created disease within the body.

Magdalene's archetypes include the Divine Feminine. The Sophia (Wisdom Deity), the Embodied Mother Goddess, the Bride of Christ, the Envied Companion of the Savior, and the negative energies hide it.

For that reason, Mary Magdalene was labeled an evil woman, a slut, or a prostitute. but she never was. These labels have been given to her by those who had motives discredited, were a threat to the churches, the rich, and the Negative energies controlling the people on the planet. She survived the judgment, and she is now more loved and accepted than ever.

Today, the rich will no longer eat the poor.

Like in the Bible, $100,000 a month for every eligible adult, eleven years, more than $13 million per citizen, issued directly through the satellite QFS system, every birth certificate tied to a stolen trust, now is unlocked. The Vatican's ancient treasures in underground vaults and ghost accounts abroad are being returned to those they defrauded. The global pay structure has been adjusted. Social security will soar to $5,000, or perhaps more. This is the rebalancing of civilization.

This is not imagination, this is reparation. Those who have planned this theft will face the consequences in a military court. At that point, the vision stopped.

CHAPTER 2
The Hidden Code

The voice came in the middle of the night while I was dreaming. I was on a hill, looking down at the view of the Pacific Ocean. The most beautiful lagoon that exists.

This is something that we can't allow to happen at this time, said a male voice. We have entered a new Era. We are moving into a higher level. On a soul level, they, the people, can tell. At the subconscious level, they will know, but not on a conscious level, because people are thinking of physical energy. The Church removed her to destroy Divine Femininity. The Famous artist who painted the Last Supper knew, so he coded it as a warning. His painting had the power to annihilate the falsehood of every religious Institution on Earth. Like an ancient mystery school coded it in symbols. The zodiac arrangement and mysterious knowledge were buried by the Vatican.

I asked the entity, "What are you talking about? Who are you?" The voice continued, "This is why the deep state is panicking."

But who are you?, I said again.

"I am Thoth," he replied. The inventor of writing and the patron of Scribes. I came to work with your writing. For the Egyptians, I was the god of the moon, and its cycles were sometimes replaced. The sun god RA at night.. I have been associated with the concept of divine order. I am the god of wisdom, knowledge, and magic. In Greek mythology, I was associated with the god Hermes and became known as Thoth the thrice-great."

The age of Aquarius has begun, we have entered a new Era, as you know it, and the entire Zodiac has been restarted. This is why the Deep State is in panic.

Mary Magdalena is the only woman at the table in the Last Supper. She is a sign of Virgo, or the Virgin Mary, not a follower. But she is a tower of Knowledge, a High Priest, and a lost part in the Holy Spirit. The Church removed her to destroy divine femininity. Revealed by Da Vinci through divine geometry, color codes, and astrological positions.

In the painting, Jesus wears a red dress with a blue robe, and the Virgin Mary wears a Blue dress with a red robe. They represent the left and right brain. The Male and Female, Sun and Moon, Positive and Negative. The Yin and Yang. Representing the balance and the harmony in the universe. Which is balance, the secrets to unlock the sanctity consciousness.

The "Last Supper" is a layout, a preparation of paradise that has been dormant to signal a transition between eras and awaken the light of Christ within people.

The number 13 is an elite code. It is Jesus and the twelve Apostles. Thirteen bloodlines. The numbers of the rebirth and the revolution. It is a body of authority that intervenes to use sacred numbers against people.

This is the time of the great awakening, and the cabal wants you distracted, confused, asleep, because as soon as you turn on the light of Christ inside. They will fall.

Pay great attention to what I am saying now. Knowledge is power, and it gives you freedom.

CHAPTER 3
Transhumanism And The Message Coded In Your DNA

I remember it was in September of this year that my friend Mila had a vision. While in meditation, she felt she was having some type of experimental experience. She could see some beings walking around the room who seemed to be checking on the forms encapsulating her. The beings were in white doctor coats, but she did not feel they were humans. She saw machines and also holograms.

The hybrids she saw were also talking, and she heard some of their conversations.

Hybrid: "My understanding is that another white coat, the healer, gets in touch with the energy of the entity that is being healed on a more immediate basis. It's the ability to expand their aura, to reach out and touch other individuals. It allows a book-up over what seems to be the time and space. It is a question of utilizing the pathways surrounding all humans' electrical kind of a sense of forcefield, an energized area around each. It simply seeks out the problem areas and dissolves them. Then the healer removes the blocks and allows subjects to regain healthy conditions."

We are actually at a pivotal moment. This is a lifetime when many will be led into the new world. And this is why the God Duo, CHADD and VIE, was sent to help you connect with the divine, with the consciousness of All that Is.

We, CHADD and VIE, are here to set up a new way of living, with a new kind of experience. A new way of existing between lifetimes. So that the cycle of pain does not begin. For you to be more aware of their reasons for living, less intoxicated by the myth of pain, you will be. The less you will be with the idea that learning must come through pain. You deserve to know the truth.

Every cell in the body vibrates to its frequency, interacting with other cells. There is a coded message inside your DNA, and there is a growing movement from the dark in control of the planet to replace your bodies with technology. You deserve to know the truth. Right now, the Shuman resonance is completely off the chart; we don't know when it will end. Many people on Earth can't sleep, and others have cardiac problems or anxiety.

I decided to find more details concerning this concern, and I received the answer.

Divinity is a force that transcends human capability. Divinity has nothing to do with religion, and this growing movement wants to erase the teachings of the Essenes.

"The Essenes believed in the laws of Moses. They had an apocalyptic view of punishment for sins and believed in the coming Messiah. They believed the present evil age was ending and a new Kingdom would be established. They believed in immortality. The Essenes had a strong belief in justice and removed themselves from the general society into their communities.

The idea of Divinity is very closely tied to the idea of transcendence. It means going beyond perceived limitations. It means growing this natural, organic quality of humanity that empowers you to confront your fears and become a greater version of yourself.

Human DNA functions as a fractal antenna in electronic fields. In every cell of your human body lies a tiny bit of DNA, which acts as an antenna that can receive signals from the surrounding environment. It acts just like antennas in your cell phones that are always kept on and always receiving human inspiration and intuition and are always receiving inspiration from the surrounding electromagnetic fields produced by nature.

Your biology was built for this through millions of years of evolution.

There is a growing movement by the elites to replace our bodies with technology. These people think the machines they make are more capable than the people who make them. However, the computer chip is limited by the physics of which it is made, and the physical space between atoms of silicon is how they rank the efficiency of the Central Processing Unit. But the upper limit of the human neuron is not known, and every time it reaches its capacity, the human neuron adapts and becomes faster and stronger. They have to build a faster one each time. That is the power of your divine internal technology. It upgrades itself as it works. This unique quality is inherent only in biological life. Some forces in the world resist this truth, and instead of fostering unity, they focus on amplifying division, emphasizing differences in ways that create fear and uncertainty. Instilling fear and leading people to believe they are broke and powerless. This fear creates a cycle where technology is presented as a solution but often ends up reinforcing dependence. It is a pattern that keeps us passive and disconnected from our true potential.

But when fear is replaced with understanding and connection, you rediscover your freedom, the freedom of love that creates and shapes your destiny as an active participant in this extraordinary universe. By raising your vibration and reconnecting with the wisdom within, you can transcend these limitations and embrace the infinite potential that is your birthright.

I heard a beep on my phone telling me I received a text. I have just arrived. It was Mat letting me know we needed to meet. I hurried up, dressed, went to his dad, where he was for the day, and picked him up.

Mat became autistic after receiving vaccinations and can drive, but he has had 3 car accidents. Luckily, he was not hurt, but being under-prescribed psychotropic drugs, he decided not to buy another car. It was too dangerous for him and others.

We were going to go to church but had to change plans and went to sit around the lake instead. The weather was great, and the water was clear and still. We heard the birds and enjoyed the stillness when we saw a Sarasota County Command Police Truck with a huge round camera on the back. It went to park in a parking lot not far from us, behind a restaurant building, and we lost sight of it, though we knew it was parked there. Around twenty-five minutes later, we heard a man's voice I immediately recognized.

This was the voice of a man who, every day when I walk, goes back and forth around the lake, talking nonsense. I concluded that the man went to war, lost his mind, and his leg. And I found out today it was not the case.

I looked in the direction from which the voice came in but did not see him. Instead, I saw the Command police truck coming back to view and leaving. I heard the man in the voice say, " God bless you" and leave. On the back of his T-shirt was written in big letters, Jesus.

I wondered what it was about, and I realized that since I met Mat, peculiar incidents had happened. The first event was in the church's parking lot. From the car, before getting out, I could see a bird acting unusually. I entered the Chapel, and here was sitting inside, this woman with dark energy. The second time was after visiting the Monastery, I stopped with Mat to take a bite, and a man poisoned my food. And now this happened when I was around the lake.

Twenty-four hours later, my family was threatened by Katherine, the surrogate archon. She has already made it impossible for us to meet for six months and now she does not want us to communicate at all, so she threatened my family, and all this was orchestrated by her.

When the Checkerboard represents M-K Ultra. Satan is jealous and hates CHADD, thus using the harsh woman and her corrupted son, Paul. They want to stop him and keep him captive. That is what the real conflict is.

Words are swift to slander and destroy, but facts are truth takes more time, except...once a lie is believed, very few and intelligent people will consider another version of what they were illegitimately fed!

But that time, my family began to see the Truth. The Truth will come to Light. Katherine and Paul's lies are beginning to come to light, and karma will catch them.

CHADD sat silently for a moment, then whispered, "Hang by the tongue."

CHAPTER 4
The Transhuman Movement
Dreamed By Emily

There is always a desire to know everything that is out there with Emily. Emily is a nineteen-year-old girl. Emily has her wishes for many things at the same time. She just needs to know that everything she wishes to experience she already has, and that the desire to experience everything is being fulfilled.

But that time, it was an experience in a dream for her protection.

Emily was shown the transhumanism replacing human biology with technology.

Emily saw the creation of the first chip destined to interface with the human brain, where the neurons are interfacing with the chip to connect the human brain to the hard drive of a computer. She thought it was fascinating and cool at first, as it connects with no physical connection or wires, like Bluetooth, and thoughts become manifest.

"This is so cool, I can play a game without touching the keywords says Emily, talking to a group of friends with her in the dream."

But that is where she heard a voice that scared her and discouraged her from trying. The voice says: "Listen, young lady, it is not for fun or cool at all. You have not been told, or you have not discovered yet, about the relationship with your body and how rare the human potential really is.

This is the takeover of your brain, and there is no turning back after. This is an extremely dangerous piece of an instrument to take away people's consciousness.

You need to know, Emily, that there exists a group of dark entities. They cannot create like you can with your mind, so they want to still your brain and use it to create for their own purpose, and you do not want that."

When Emily awakened from her dream, she was in shock at the vision. She picked up her phone and spoke to all her friends in her dream and told them everything. She explained in detail what she saw.

CHAPTER 5
The Three Types Of Med Beds

Before the home COVID test kit was sold, the only way to be tested was in care centers and hospitals. At that time, free speech was not allowed, and fake news was keeping humans in fear. I was considered a conspirator. I could not be heard and was not trusted, and I was forced to take the test in one of these facilities administering these kinds of tests if I wanted to come home. The nurse pushed and twisted so hard inside my nose that it destroyed my protection and introduced a nasty virus into my body.

I knew, then, the only way to heal was to find a cure from somewhere other than a Medical doctor with a degree from Big Pharma, and I finally came into contact with a group from Zeta Reticula. I knew it would only come from another planet than Earth. It is that group that exists in the Universe, powerful and famous for its healing facility, that came forward to help me. The Zetians. They know how to heal all energy levels and different people from different races. Not only on Gaia's plan but also on other planets.

So, after 3 years of suffering and searching, I encountered a Zeta Reticula group and one Zetian in particular. I also wanted to hear about the real MedBeds. So many fake MedBeds were out and advertised to the people. I heard some of them mark the people with the mark of the beast. So, I asked the Zetians. And this is how I received directly from the group the explanation of the MedBeds becoming so popular.

"There are three types of Med Beds: (These are all the types of med beds, the natural way of healing the body.) The moment the world has been waiting for.

1. The ALOCENTRIC BED. (Regenerative.) It is Allopathic Energy stimulating the cells to grow and reproduce organs and parts of the body missing. It regenerates tissues and body parts. It is an energy moving in all directions. A sort of soundwave pattern. Immune systems like lupus erythematosus and rheumatoid arthritis cause patients pain, but stem cell therapy easily "tames" them. Stem cells work miracles. Immune system diseases surrender.

2. The HOLOGRAPHIC BED. It works on bio-location. On a parallel life to heal the body. Revitalize, renew, and restore.

3. The GRAPHIS BED. (Re-atomization Med Beds. The fountain of youth) In 2 or 3 minutes, the whole body, head to toe. This advanced technology means that an 80-year-old woman could be 30 years old again in 3 minutes. Now she can have children again and a whole new family if she wants. A technology of a perpetual fountain of youth. It purifies the body to heal. Crystalline and gemstone energy, Light, and Colors to heal.

The military seized over ten thousand MedBeds from the deep-state bunkers. The Global Elite is in panic as MedBeds Healing Centers are activated. The facilities are secured by the military, where trafficked children and war heroes are being healed first. Suppressed and hidden technology is finally in the hands of people.

The MedBeds were hidden for decades in classified underground military bases controlled by corrupted intelligence factions. US Space Force and white hat divisions secured within forty-eight hours, and they received an order to seize five major MedBeds set for destruction. The mission received by the US military was to deploy the MedBeds, heal the innocent, and expose the truth.

The deep state attempted to sabotage a MedBed facility in Arizona by firebombed. Days later, a shipment was intercepted in Texas but recovered by the special forces. Then, an EMP attack targeted a training center in Florida. Each attempt failed, and MedBeds remains operational.

They are already healing those who suffered the most. Thousands of trafficked children, rescued from underground facilities, are receiving treatment. Brain trauma is erased, and internal injuries are healed. It is years of abuse that are undone. Soldiers who fought to dismantle deep state networks are being restored.

They confirmed my intuition that Big Pharma is leading to the emergency broadcast (EBS) activation. When it goes live, the world will see the truth.

The mainstream media will go dark, and the military will reveal the deep state's crimes."

Then I heard another voice saying: MED BED is a tool, not a necessity. A new wave of healing is returning.

The Healing wave does not need a Med Bed. It is already working for you. It is reversing symptoms, restoring memories, and reconnecting your soul to your body.

Start now, do not wait. When you feel it, whether with warmth, peace, or the release of past pain, you are silently understanding what others discover.

The archives reveal a forgotten truth. The first MedBed did not appear in the twenty-first century, but in 1936. In a secret laboratory, a small group of physicists and biologists began evaluating the concept of cell regeneration using frequency.

The results were very impressive. Wounds closed in a record time, and inflammation is almost instantly way. The damaged nerves showed signs of restoration previously considered impossible.

But what could have become a medical was instead silenced. The discovery was stamped as classified and handed to the military rather than being shared with the world.

From that moment on, technology was buried, hidden from the public's eyes and preserved only for those in power.

CHAPTER 6
A New Era has Begun You Have Been Awakened

I was shelf browsing in a library when the person, a military man, next to me began to talk and said:

"MedBeds, It is Happening Now! It is the Med Bed revolution, and the final collapse of Big Pharma. Med Beds GESARA. DNA regeneration, regression, limp regrowth, cancer erased, Autism reversed, PTSD healed, organs rebuilt. It is military tech being rolled out now under the protection of the White Hats.

The plan is that soon every big city will have treatment centers, not hospitals. The outdated medical center system is over. Virtually all hospital procedures will be outdated. Almost all hospital procedures will become obsolete within a year. No VIP line, no insurance, only culling. Dying people with disabilities and children tortured in tunnels will go first. For the Priority to Vaccinated, and the

Priority to Veterans, they have been treated from outer space.

This is the future, and it is happening now. The New Wave of Healing rebuilds the severed spine, reverses serious disease, repairs brain damage, grows new organs, removes chemotherapy damage, restores genetic purity, and reduces your age to 30 years.

They can heal your soul, heal your mental wounds. If you are not ready to let go of pain, quantum technology will know.

The bed sees everything. Low mood denies access or needs counseling. You can't pretend to be ready. The bed sees everything.

The National Hotline will open, you will call, will be scanned. Quantum computers will assess the urgency and allocate you to the center. No discrimination, only demand.

It will be run by Military medical teams trained by benevolent aliens. Not by large pharmaceutical companies. The treatment center will be separated from corrupt hospitals. Those will be canceled. GESARA is the funding source, free for everyone.

Large pharmaceutical companies are dying. A new era has begun."

He asked me if I had any questions he could answer, then left.

I am so used to it now. I just listen and wait until it makes sense. And it always finally makes sense.

CHAPTER 7
The Central Crystal

Earth is a graduating school with strong souls. Earth is a tough school. Other civilizations learn from it; other civilizations don't have the same degree.

It was early morning, and I was walking fast inside the convention center I had just entered. I had to register, find my booth's location, and set it up before the public started coming. I knew by experience that once they pass the booth, if I am not ready, they rarely come back. Not that the person is not interested, but more distracted by other booths, and maybe attending some lectures and forgetting to come back.

I was just finishing and nearly ready when the first person came for a quick 15-minute session. And for the following hour, the public kept coming. I made one session after another. My energy was already very high when I took a look at the room around me and saw a crowd looking attentively at what I was doing. They were attracted by the glow and the peace my light energy was creating in people.

It was the turn of an eighteen-year-old girl. She sat nervously on the chair. I asked her to relax, get comfortable, close her eyes, put her hands on her lap and just forget about everything. And she did. I concentrated on my work and was about to finish balancing her body. She was reflecting peace and joy on her face. I even saw tears of joy dropping down her cheeks when, suddenly, her name was Sandra, she opened her eyes and said:

Oh! My God! Wow! I can hear the radio very clearly. What happened?

Here is what happened, I said, the human structure is crystalline in a geometric form, and I cleaned and completely rebalanced your body with my crystalline light and sacred geometry.

Earth is a graduating school with strong souls. Earth is a tough school. Other civilizations learn from it. Other civilizations don't have the same degree.

In the days of the Lemurian and Atlantean eras, extraterrestrials brought a crystal to this planet through dimensional portals.

From deep underground, beneath the Himalayan mountains, was a giant central crystal containing an awareness of higher knowledge of the Earth and its inhabitants. The central crystal had been inside the Earth for thousands of years. Crystals communicate with all the pathways of the system and all the crystals on the planet. With everything and everyone carrying a crystal structure, the crystal consciousness is in it.

The crystal communicates with your DNA. Because your DNA has crystals in its structure, the center crystal is transparent. As you connect with its consciousness, the spaces open to the world of crystal consciousness, and then it will feel that it is in this crystal space. This central crystal, which stores all the knowledge of man and the universe, can communicate with you now, and especially in sacred and energetic places, is energetically connected with the crystal through the crystal.

To all who are awake and ready: The great shift is coming.

Thousands of giant triangular crystals placed by the galaxy will rise from the ground at the time of the great shift.

The light is healing, and the spirit will allow each soul to transform its consciousness and form into an upgraded body, and each soul will immediately grow. In the inner world.

The young eighteen years old girl, after having her experience, said: Master Adama is the High Priest of the sacred Lemurian city of Telos, located beneath Mount Shasta, California. He is the head of the Lemurian Council of Light and is considered a leader in spiritual guidance and ascension. Adama is also portrayed as a representative of a future, ascended humanity.

Master Adama prepares to make the first contact with those "ready" and leads the surface humans into the light chamber to transform into full consciousness.

She hugged me and left.

CHAPTER 8
Reincarnation And Pathlife

Recently, I have been going to places I have rarely been before. I deeply go into transcendent experiences with a sense of magic and mystery. As I progressed, I brought back information, but nothing could explain it.

Some other realms with vivid and powerful scenes. All your lives are happening right now. Simultaneously. The belief system in which you are stuck is an illusion. Nobody is stuck in reincarnation on this planet. It is linked to the idea of reincarnation.

When you make a choice, then are consequences of those choices.

Everything you do is some type of choice. So, some type of belief system or some type of perspective. You must understand it regarding the actual nature of space and time.

You can listen to the loud and irrational social media influences overreacting, or you can use your intuition and begin to cooperate. The choice is yours.

Reincarnation is a misnomer because time is an illusion.

There is no past, no future. There is only now. So, what you call past lives, reincarnation, etc., is simultaneous multiple concurrent incarnations all going on now, but in different frequencies and wavelengths, so you do not perceive one another. It is like a multitude of programs happening all at the same time, but you turn to one at that moment and you do not perceive the others until you change to another channel.

All your lives are happening at the same time.

The Past, the Present, and the Future.

Physical reality is just a dream that you are having. Life is a dream. You have never left spirit. It is your natural state. You are in spirit right now, but you are dreaming that you are not.

Jesus understood it and expanded the consciousness beyond the physical parameters to a certain point. To allow a fuller expression of his total being of all that is to surface through, as all of you can do.

That was actually Jesus teaching:

"Greater things that I have done will you do"

Page 32

CHAPTER 9
Sent To Another Assignment

While CHADD and its path are still filled with trauma, tribulation, and triumph.

I am sent to another assignment. I look around and see I am in a chamber inside a ship, but a different one this time. The people on board the spaceship want you to know it is space technology. I am a channel; all I do is transmit the information given to me to you.

"Many of you are having sleep disorders during this time, and that is because the Galactic Federation is constantly following your progress and is in touch with you telepathically. Giving you instructions on their landing and further connections with you. They are glad that many of you have progressed and are more aligned with the central sun, meaning the fifth dimension. And we are also happy to be of assistance to all. Expect it soon.

You are loved and protected. You're special and unique. Just open your hearts and let the Light in.

Some of you are blocking the Light in. Set the intention to let the Light pass through all your hurts, through all your traumas. The Light will heal you when you allow everything to surface for healing.

You must not confuse religion and spirituality. Due to human imperfection, religion has become corrupt, politically divisive, and a tool for power struggles. Spirituality is not ideology or theology. It is a simple way of living, pure and original as given by the Highest. God. Spirituality is a network linking us to our Creator, the Universe, and each other. "

God is the electromagnetic pulse of energy that gives life and life within all living things.

CHAPTER 10
From The Feminine Realm: The Sacred Feminine Archetype

In this time of Lent, I began to receive complex images. I had to contact Gaby, residing in Madrid, which led me to contact Zara in London. Something big was about to happen.

The sacred feminine archetype is widely known all over the world and is the central figure of worship within the Christian Catholic faith. Known as the Blessed Virgin Mary, our Lady, and Queen of Heaven. Mother of God. She is known as Maryam in Islam. The Chosen One or Purified One. Mother Mary has been worshipped as a Mother Goddess throughout the Christian era. Mother Mary has always been revered as a symbol of the Great Mother and known for her unconditional love. And forgiveness.

The feminine essence is linked to the heart center. The heart is the most powerful magnetic energy. But the war's suppression of the feminine energy system has made it harder for women these days to be comfortable with expressing their feelings. Women are often chastised and ridiculed for being overwhelmed for centuries when they show deep emotion and experience the cleansing feelings to move and breathe.

I saw myself dressed in white, sitting in the middle of crystals. I enjoy the energy moving through my body. It is energizing and very peaceful, calming at the same time. I feel the frequency of the crystals around me. This place is in the mountains. I listen to nature. I have gone there to gather the energy that I use for people. I collect it and take it with me. I found this special place with the crystals when I was young. Suddenly, I felt drawn to a woman. She is also sitting in the middle of a circle and surrounded by crystals. She seemed different. There is something different about her. She reads my mind, laughs, and says I am a spirit. We exchanged a few words, and she continued:

"I am a spirit. I am part of a group; we go to places and help people and then we come back and share another mission. We volunteer. Sometimes the places we go to are more difficult than others. The difficulty is that we are cut off from the collective, and we have to remember our mission.

The door closes behind us, and we just have to remember. The veil that lets us through is thick again, and we only have what we bring with us. We have to train and make sure the people we came to help are aware. If they open up to the energy, they can hear, feel, and understand.

When someone comes to awareness, they will find themselves more compassionate and loving without experiencing in return. The relationship with Christ Jesus is very personal. No one and nothing should control it for you. The same goes for our Mother, our relentless guide who has offered us unconditional love and support.

Mother Mary represents the ultimate compassionate witness from the Divine Feminine realm. As Mary represents the Divine Mother of Humanity, she naturally brings us awareness. When she touches us in life with her divine blue Light and activates her mantle of protection in our aura, the right emotional support figures will show up like a miracle, and just when you most need them.

Mary said: As we heal our wounds arising from the restless severance of faith in the ancient feminine, we make it easier for Earth to recover and rebalance."

And I agreed. At that moment, the Universe is calling you to align your life to a higher energetic frequency at any given moment.

According to Pleiadians, Jesus' soul is Pleiades, and his name is Sananda. He was born naturally, like other humans. His Mother, Mary's originates is the Pleiades, and her name is Sheemosa.

His father Joseph's soul name is Oupea. The actual date of birth is September eight.

The Pleiadians were part of the various ancient tribes of beings in this universe; they, along with the Arcturians, Venusians, and many others, were a higher-dimensional group with the purest intent to serve the Great Source, the Creator, wherever and whenever needed.

Fully dedicated to serving divine love in everything they do. They serve all things faithfully, with the highest good in mind.

The above alien races have been the main guardians of this Galaxy for millions of years.

The Pleiades are fully prepared for all events, and there is nothing that humans can create through fear or other third-dimensional threats that can cause damage. They will not oppose those who may be considered weapons; neither will they do anything that could be misconstrued as deliberately antagonizing mankind. Pleiades communicate with each other through telepathy and can communicate with you in any language in the world.

This highly developed race of beings radiates a powerful, high energy of love and light that will make you feel safe, comfortable, loved and truly loved. They remain one of the guardians protecting humanity in this galaxy.

They play an important role in the spiritual awakening and development of the human species. They have risen from a lower dimension to a higher dimension of consciousness, the fifth and higher dimensions, millions of years from your world.

At Christmastime time remember the teacher who taught that God is only found within you. When people saw the stars moving in the sky, like the star of Bethlehem, they were seeing Galactic Federation crafts. Many messengers have come.

All Gaby remembered was that she said she heard "noons" from a German man, and for Zara, she said she kept having me back again on her mind. She knew we had to meet for more.

Hum! That was another mystic encounter! I thought. Let's see what is coming.

I still have to meet Zara. She said she should be contacting me to meet. I am saying should because things move so fast.

CHAPTER 11
Leaving the Material World And Entering The Age Of Frequency

In this new age time of enlightenment, the journey to the unknown, and the quest for Self-Mastery with the God Duo on an Earth mission, at the beginning there was Katherine the harsh worker like my star family named her, and then came Agnes the spy who reported everything she learned, saw, and heard from me, and came Mike the friend of a friend of a Pastor named Young who both tried to kill CHADD. I am not sure yet where Mike fits in. I have been advised to be very careful.

Satan enlisted the loyalty of the secret societies to conspire to teach a theology of the world that is contrary to the Biblical one. Rosicrucians and Freemasons translated the Bible to control the world.

And then came the time when all changed. Now they are all frustrated. They can't stop the sound of the Trumpet, they can't stop the five-dimensional ascension process, and they can't stop the liberation and my new living timeline.

We are leaving the Age of material and entering the Age of frequency. The Universe is abundant in energy. It has no beginning and no end.

I had just finished visiting Atlanta and meeting with my friend Alma. We had spent a night at a beautiful hotel. We got up in the morning and were packing to go to the airport to return home. Our flight was forty-five minutes different in departure. I was waiting in front of my gates when a lady sitting next to me received a phone call. She hung up and began to speak to me.

In this exciting and original view of the Universe, VIE, you give an inspiring picture of an expanded, conscious, holistic Universe. Showing that our bodies mirror the Universe's pulsating, vibrational Universe. Our brains are thought amplifiers, and the Universe is a hologram interpreting a holographic Universe, and so is the human brain.

You are right, claiming their truth will ease the journey. They have lost their connection to their higher mind and their intuitive abilities. They must not be afraid to admit they were misled.

By tuning their resonant frequency, they could access their higher expression and tap into the unified field of creation."

Talking of energy, frequency, and vibration, the harsh woman knows she is very sick and about to leave this Earth, and I received a very concerning phone call from CHADD. She is resisting as much as she can and is trying to drain CHADD's energy. She sold her car and is now driving his, letting him think she was going to buy a new car, but instead she now wants him to sell his. She wants him trapped in the house with her. What an archon!

That is when I heard:

"Tonight, when you are about to sleep and you will be lying down on your bed, it is a good time to speak to Mother Mary. She will be listening to you."

CHAPTER 12
Wise Vibration: The Law of Attraction

In the middle of last night, during my sleep, I heard myself saying:

Trust, have faith, and access Christ's consciousness. Twenty faces: ICOSAHEDRON. Instigate dimensional transport, twelve, DEDOCAHEDRON METATRON's CUBE/Flower of Life represents Male and Female, to create an Oneness field, all there is. 5-POINTED STARS, Ascension. Then you begin to access Christ's Consciousness. (The drive for Universal Motorization).

- Yellow, health, the body
- White, the body
- Green, healing
- Violet, transformation, and protection

I am aware of angels around me. It's the most beautiful place I think of. I am shown how to protect myself. They just took me to show me the feeling and the protection, and the love. Then I went immediately to a place where there was nothing but the white Light.

I am hearing CHADD now saying, "Do you remember what happened to me when I went into a coma? I was told not to look at it directly. Embrace it, but do not stare at it."

Wow! Hum! You are here, too, my blue flame, I said. So, we are going through this event together again.

CHADD: You know it, always. Ok, you have no attachment, go for it and begin the session. This session will be a bit longer. We have to apply the protocol we have just been guided to, and also, we have to take time to inform and teach Judy. She is ready for it. Our client Judy wants to learn about the law of attraction.

I spaced out at this point, busy applying the protocol, to hear me back talking again. To Judy at that time.

"What you put out is what you get back. Reality is a mirror. Let me explain it to you. What you call the Law of attraction, in many ways, is your vibration that creates your reality. But there is also something else, it is about that concept that many of you are either missing or overlooking. Because while it is true that whatever your vibration is, it is responsible for what you experience.

Many of you think or have been taught to think that you have to work to create that vibration that would attract what it is you prefer, and you do not. Your core frequency and core true signature vibration are already attracting all the things that are representative of that core vibration.

If these things that are representative of the true loving creative natural vibration are not manifesting and are not reaching you, it is not because you are not attracting them. It is because you are keeping them away.

That is the difference. Because everything that is representative of that core frequency is doing its best to get to you. If it cannot reach you, it is because you are keeping it away. With your definitions, your beliefs, and your ideas about not being worthy of it.

Everything that is not compatible with your vibration. It is doing its best to get as far away from you as it possibly can. But if it does not leave you, if it is hanging around, and it is not what you prefer, it is not because it can't, in that sense, represent your vibration. It is because you are holding on to it. So, the idea of the law of attraction, in one sense, is accurate.

It is more about letting go of these things that don't work for you and letting go of those things. And that is how the law of attraction works.

I will conclude by saying, stay on the path you are on. Keep trying, keep working."

CHAPTER 13
The Launching of a Massive Operation

I had no problem getting into a trance. I am floating, and it feels so comfortable and beautiful. It looks like I am looking at the Universe.

A man giving a lecture at a convention asks for the right answer. Is there a point when we stop?

What is he asking? I do not believe so, because everything is energy, and energy never dies. There is no end to the energy.

Then I felt pulled down and entered a chamber. It's like you enter the chamber, and important pieces of information are provided.

CHADD and I will be transmitting the knowledge, said the man.

"Schools shouldn't be talking to kindergarteners about their gender identity. Or they should be arrested for it. But the dark energies worshipping Lucifer are violating federal orders to halt the insane transgender assault on our children.

They should teach the children and the kids to read before telling them to go trans. They are manipulating and grooming children, and their goal is to create an entire generation of gender-confused individuals. And the media is silent. The fake establishment refuses to lift a finger.

The man continues, and CHADD and VIE are called to help.

How many more children need to be abused and indoctrinated before "We the People" bring the full force down on them?

So, this is our plan:

This will be the largest operation of its kind ever in the country's history. We are launching a nationwide operation to hunt down and replace funded school board members who indoctrinate children and have defied executive orders.

But only if we can rely on you. You have to get on board, too. You see, we are battling against the richest, evilest, and most radical men on Earth for your children and the generation to come.

One Hundred Billion Medical Scam used to destroy your metabolism. The cabal has used

Ceramides to ruin your immune system. Excess ceramide accumulation, particularly during conditions like obesity, can disrupt metabolism by impairing insulin sensitivity, promoting inflammation, and affecting mitochondrial function, potentially leading to metabolic disorders like type 2 diabetes and cardiovascular disease. Ceramides attenuate cell survival signaling and metabolic pathways while activating apoptotic mechanisms, making them tumor-suppressive. Ceramide accumulates in tissues during obesity, and how an increase in intracellular ceramide impacts cellular signaling and function.

Stop ignoring the sky. Chemtrails in the sky are designed to control, infect, and destroy!

You're in a battlefield.

The Sky reclaim project is underway. The sky is not falling, but it is being retaken.

The red-wing states have stopped waiting. The war on geoscience engineering has become a reality.

A team is currently sending a clandestine force composed of former military pilots, satellite analysts and whistleblowers to take down the globalization groups' chemical spray network. Their evidence is satellite imagery, leaks, contracts, and atmospheric tests.

An unmarked fleet of aircraft carriers continues to release toxins into the atmosphere. This is not climate engineering. It is a biological warfare, not against foreign invaders, but against you. And this under the banner of "Climate Safety. You inhale monoaluminium, barium, strontium and synthetic fillers designed to weaken you from within.

Cancer was ever natural but was engineered to kill you. They are pumping ceramides into your body to create disease and feed their Biopharmaceutical Empire.

It was never about genetics, calories, and eating an unhealthy diet, but a deliberate biochemical ambush. Each molecule is created to destroy your metabolism system, your immunity.

Ceramides are not poisons. They are used as weapons.

Genetically modified crops, seed oil, toxic skin care products, contaminated water, all that was never "modern life" but some attacks against your health. It was global medical concentration camps disguised as nutrition advice.

Your blood has become a crime scene. The fat fillers strangle your pancreas, poison the liver, trigger cancer, and destroy your body inside out. Behind closed doors, some people in white robes created a feedback cycle of destruction.

They created a disease to sell you drugs and repeat it until death. Until it kills you.

Do you know that:

Autism is a frequency, not a disorder. Schizophrenia is not a disease. It is a spiritual gift that is misfiring. They are actually tuning in multiple dimensions at one time without the support to ground them. They see people behind the veil and hear real voices. They need tools to restore coherence, grounding, and energetic shielding. Their soul by shield is fragmented. They are channels wide open and shield fragmented, and a highly sensitive empath.

Alzheimer's is not memory loss. It is a lost connection with the soul. Before the symptoms happen, the higher mind, your 3D to 6th-dimensional soul frequencies, stop flowing into the 3D brain. The light begins to dim, and the will to leave slowly fades. The disconnection is fueled by chemicals, heavy metals, radiation, unprocessed traumas, grief, fear, and betrayal. Losing sole purpose and forgetting why you are here."

You were poisoned on purpose." Well, that is what the man says.

CHAPTER 14
The Most Powerful State-of-the-Art Golden Dome Defense Shield

I receive images of the most ambitious initiative. It started with a hole, an opening going down to the Earth in an underground city. I entered a place with a group of people. They told me they had difficulty adjusting to the violence and volunteered out of love and desire to help, even though their adjustment has been difficult underground. Here is what I heard and the information I have received from them. The information on an ambitious initiative and project is being put in place. They are preparing for the future.

The Commander-in-Chief spoke:

"You are now being allowed to have the information because it is time to acknowledge who they are and their purpose on Earth at this time of great awakening.

As a Five-star General and commander-in-chief, my focus is on building the most powerful military of the future. Because everyone thinks it's glamorous to be a great soldier, but it is not.

The man. The five-star General in command now went into a trance. He consciously remembered. His conscious mind also wanted to maintain control because he was afraid, he would make up something, and all he could see was in his field of vision, the red color. It was horrible with all the killing and the blood. So many are being killed.

Then he continued saying; As a first step, I am asking the Congress to fund a State-of-the-art Golden Dome defense shield to protect our homeland.

A nationwide Golden Dome missile defense shield to protect the homeland. A Golden Dome capable of intercepting ballistic crews and hypersonic missiles before they strike any places of our great and peaceful Nation. Unfortunately, some other countries do not want peace as we do. They refuse peace and prefer war for profit.

This ambitious project Golden Dome Shield, marks a significant shift in our military strategy, aiming to counter emerging threats from China,

Russia, and others. It is a potentially rivaling Manhattan Project. "

I came out of the room, and this information, once it had been placed within me, gave me some background to relate to.

The new technology is here.

The victory for the First Amendment is not over. I see allies like Germany and Italy are cracking down on free speech in completely draconian ways, arresting people for daring to state opinions their government does not like.

Could this Dome also be a healing Dome?

CHAPTER 15
The Vaccine Empire: GAVI

My encounter with a time traveler came about unexpectedly. He knew as one can only dream of. The being began to talk to me and announced he was from the future, and I was told that this is how the information he would give me comes from.

"The people are awake, and the system is cracking. There is a cloud; it looks like it's a time-released one, and it triggers other things. So, when these Earthly events happen, they trigger a program inside humans, the ones who came in for this mission.

People will not be ruled by or obey the billionaires in lab coats, or answer to Geneva. The Vaccine Alliance GAVI has its main headquarters and secretariat in Geneva, Switzerland. All funding has just been cut, and the Globalist Health Grid is beginning to collapse. All funding to GAVI is terminated.

Gavi is an international organization created in 2000 to improve access to new and underused vaccines for children living in the world's poorest

The cartel's cash flow is now severed. Gavi, the globalist-run vaccine alliance, the WHO, and the WEF have been leeching billions off the citizen taxpayers. Sold to the public as "health aid", it has been fronted to medical tyranny, digital surveillance, and global population control. For years, people were unknowingly financing their medical enslavement. Billions pumped into a cartel that crushed free speech, censored doctors, and rewarded Big Pharmaceutical companies with blank checks while silencing dissent." Then he disappears as he comes.

It was when I left my body and entered a Monastery and saw a Monk walking in my direction. He came to welcome me.

"What can I do for you?" he warmly said. I suppose you came here so early for a reason."

Yes, indeed, I reply. I drove to the Monastery because I needed some clarification concerning the Four Angels to be released.

"Very well, I am Father Peter. By the way, let me explain. So, now the time has arrived for the Four Angels to be released.

These Four Angels were released to kill. It is happening, and there is no escape from it. These are the Four Empires that ruled the Israelite nation.

Beginning with the Assyrian Empire, followed by the Babylonian Empire, followed by the Persian Empire, and the fourth is the Median Empire (the Medes), a political entity centered in Ecbatana, existing from the seventh century BC until the mid-6th century BC. Media empires are large, multinational corporations that dominate the media landscape, controlling content creation, distribution, and consumption across various platforms, influencing programming, and shaping global culture.

These Empires were the Empires that ruled the Israelite nation at that time. They were released to kill one-third of Mankind. And this will happen no matter what. It will happen to some unfortunate, but it is happening, and there is no escape from it, no matter how much you pray. You will never be able to convince them to do it another way."

CHAPTER 16
Biblical Angels

Another day, another experience. I am seeing some double-handled doors, and I am opening these doors. I am walking into a past life to find answers. There is a huge staircase going up. Inside, there is a lot of light. There are seats. I am in a Dome that holds records and meeting places. It's like a place to access information or talk to somebody. It is an inter-dimensional temple. It is a sacred place for people to meet and have a safe place to talk.

And now there is a woman appearing with long blond hair and smelling like fresh cut flowers. She is smiling. She says that she is coming from the Pleiades. She speaks to me telepathically.

"Hello, VIE. My name is Celeste. Many are still confused about 5D Ascension because confused people are teaching. It aligns the teachings of Jesus with ancient prophecies. It's roughly aligned with the cycle, but the shift itself isn't caused by a solar flash or cosmic cycle.

It is a plan by the Galactic Federation, also known as Biblical Angels. It is not just a change of consciousness. We will blink to a new Earth. No one has gone yet. We will go together with children and pets. Evil will be left behind, and this Earth will get darker.

Sheen will be a paradise and a Galactic civilization with full disclosure, open contact, and much more. Pleiadians assure us it will happen for the generations who are alive now. We will not know when, but everyone alive can make it."

CHAPTER 17
Priestess Mary-Magdalene
And Her Blue Flame

I was getting out of my favorite coffee shop, just passed the door, when my phone rang. As I was about to cross the road, I stepped one or two steps back, making sure I could hear who this was and what the person had to say. The voice seemed to come from my back. I turned around and so a man with nice sunglasses, his phone in one hand and a coffee in the other.

He smiled, hung up his phone, and introduced himself.

I learned later, wondering who he was, how he found me, and why he needed to speak to me. His name was Liam, and he had just lost his wife to cancer.

He asked me politely to give him a little of my time to hear his story. So, we chose some seats, and I listened to him.

My wife was psychic, and so was I. I have been told to contact you, and tell you my story, and your energy while I count my story to you will help me grieve. So, he went on and told me his story. Sad one, but he could hold her hand until she had to finish the cross-over alone.

Then this was not all, he had an important message for you. It was about an exorcist Priest.

Reverend Gallican exorcist Priest Engerrand wants you to know what happened lately while doing an exorcism. He asked the demon possessing the person if there were different types of demons in possession, and the demon replied: I can't even say her name, but there is this 'woman' we are so scared of, we cannot even say her name. I immediately received the answer. It is Our Blessed Mother Mary, Queen of the Universe.

Liam went on explaining,

"The Roman Christian Church discovered that the belief in the divine feminine was so strong in some of the pagan lands that they conquered that they needed to provide some sort of replacement for the pagan Goddesses. Thus, they turned the Mother of God into an object of devotion for two reasons.

They would provide a feminine figure to be worshipped without having to acknowledge the existence of any Goddess. Thus, God and the entire Trinity could remain exclusively male.

And, by shifting the devotional focus away from Magdalene towards Mary, they could better hide the fact that Jesus had a wife who was a Priestess; it would be hard to justify their anti-Priestess policy. The anti-Priestess attitude of the Roman Catholic Church stems from the fact that the true founder of Catholicism is not Jesus but the Apostle Paul.

The Gospel of Mary-Magdalene is like a hidden cipher, a fragment of truth, but she is a leader, buried beneath centuries of silence. It is painting a picture of a woman who wasn't just a follower but a leader, entrusted with secrets Jesus shared with no one else. When you read it you feel the tension, with Peter's Jealousy, Andrew's doubt, and Mary standing firm, recounting visions of the soul's escape from the chain of the world.

It is a story that suspends everything you have been told about the early church, hitting at a sacred feminine that has been erased to consolidate the power of the dark in control since that time.

It is a rebellion against the forces that tried to bury Mary's legacy.

The Divine Light is within, and when it is recognized, it illuminates everything. Light is often symbolic of the spiritual knowledge that frees the soul. It is the uncovering of the Divine spark within everyone."

Mary-Magdalene speaks now,

"I have been chosen. I am the chosen one and the door to the divine. I am a portal. I came to infuse the Divine Feminine upon the earth, and I am that same Mary Magdalene who was with Jesus of Nazareth when He walked the earth plane. I am his other half.

We have a connection at the heart center. When the two Sacred Fires, God's Pink Flame of Divine Love and our Father God's Blue Flame of Divine Power, merge into higher frequencies of the seven solar aspects of deity, which is the fifth-dimensional crystalline Solar Violet Flame. The glorious Violet Flame predominantly influences the earth during the two-thousand-year cycle of the Aquarian Age we are now entering.

I was a high Priestess, highly skilled in the art of Sacred alchemy. I hold in my DNA the Divine Mother codes.

I came to do the same blessed work I did then. To teach, guide you and work as a Vibration Intuitive

Energy, the Light has come with Sound, and Love leads the way."

I said, Thank you, Liam. Love, Light, Peace, and Blessings.

I learned a few months after we met that he had moved out of his house and gone to live in the mountains in Central America doing charity work.

CHAPTER 18
Sananda Group, Ascending Beings, The Christ Consciousness

This was a most unusual and lucid experience. I arrived at the destination somewhat exhausted and lay down for a rest. Upon relaxing, I drifted out, and I was floating. The vibrations came in. Suddenly, a man appeared in front of me. I got an impression of calm and strength. He looked at me and asked: Do you know why I am here? I am called James. Then his hand placed a book before my closed eyes. The book was opened, and I saw both printed pages.

I said to James: May I? Then I began to read.

Jesus, Sananda, Yeshua, is part of high frequency Soul collective known as the Sananda group. It is not just a name but a Soul title, a vibrational signature representing a group of ascending beings who carry the Christ consciousness template across dimensions of lifetimes.

Yeshua came to Earth physical embodiment of Christ energy, not to start a religion but to awaken remembrance. His mission was to anchor the frequencies of divine love, forgiveness, unity consciousness, and Soul resurrection. He did not act alone. He was supported by many beings in the Galactic Federation, the white brotherhood, and especially the Syrian and the Pleiadian Councils. These Soul groups have been involved in Earth's evolution for millennia, helping guide humanity through key shifts.

So, yes, Yeshua is part of the Sananda stream, and through him, that consciousness entered the Earth plane to help trigger a mass spiritual awakening. His life, death and resurrection were all part of Cosmic initiation, not just for himself but for humanity.

The Law of material, known as the RA material, relates directly to what Yeshua was trying to teach. The Law of One material, also known as RA material, is one of the clearest transmissions that aligns directly with what Yeshua came to teach, and their threads of the same Cosmic truth flowing from the same source just delivered different time frames and vessels.

The Core teaching of One on this issue, the true teachings before they were filtered or reshaped, were about their unity. I am the father of One, whatever you do to the least of these year you do to me. The kingdom of heaven is within you.

These are direct reflections of the Law of One, which says open all things, all beings, all life, all consciousness is One. There is no separation. All is One infinite Creator experiencing itself in the raw material; there are two paths. Service to self and service to others.

Yeshua embodied the path of service completely through healing, forgiveness, sacrifice, and unconditional love. He was not asking people to worship him. He was modeling the vibration needed to graduate into higher density, what RA calls moving from the third density to the fourth density. The realm of unconditional love.

God even refers to Yeshua as a wanderer. A being who came from higher densities to incarnate a body on Earth with the mission to serve. His Soul is coming through the sun under streams to anchor on Earth Christ Consciousness. He was a sixth-density being embodying wisdom and compassion, just like RA itself, also speaking from Sixth density.

The hands closed the book, took it away. I soared out through the door, up in the sky, and came back.

CHAPTER 19
Renewable Body of Energy, Your Body Never Dies

What I saw at first glance looked normal. Then it began to change. The extraterrestrial person I saw had been doing this for a few years.

There is a ship stationed in the sky. It is not on the ground. It's round and it is quite a large ship. It fits 200 people. Some of these people on the ship go back and forth to different parts of the planet, said the man. All of them are different, they don't wear clothes, have flesh colored, and a thin body. They don't interact with the people. They are involved with the interaction of the planets, the universal goal, harmony, and peace. They protect the planets from self-destruction. They bring Light and Love. Everyone is affected by the energy rippling through the Universe.

The being that appeared in my vision is named Astrophel and traveled from place to place to teach those who would listen. He looks different from the others on board the chip. He has a very small mouth, a big head, large eyes, and large fingers. When he is on the ship, he helps organize the teachers who go down on the planet to help.

Astrophel, as the others do not eat. They are kept alive by absorbing the Light into the body.

When the body wears out, when it has been used for a period of time, then they dispose of it and retain a new body. The body does not die. It is renewable energy. The body is not reduced to energy; the body is pure energy. It is a shape, like an outline, but it is less solid. Moving more freely about than a being that would be more in a physical form. Death is not the end; consciousness expands beyond the body. Fear is the biggest obstacle to healing and true freedom. We are already whole, already enough, already loved.

Then I was given a wonderful vision. It is a mother named Iris who had her daughter, Kira, who was in her final stage of cancer. The cancer was destroying her body she fell into a coma. The doctor told Iris that her daughter, Kira, had only a few hours to live. But instead of slipping away, Kira was given the choice: if she returned, she would be healed. She decided to return and she was healed.

Kira said she has experienced something amazing. She expanded into a vast, luminescent awareness. And said that she experienced no fear, no pain, just infinite love and the deepest sense of being home. She felt liberated and free, enveloped in a feeling of pure unconditional Love. Something beyond anything she had ever known in her life.

There is no reason to be fighting. It serves no purpose. I came here to help say Astrophel. Earth's people can live in peace and harmony. They do not have to die. The physical dying of the body came from the introduction by the cabal of chemical poisons to the bodies and the wars they created.

But there is the birth of a new planet. Many chips encircle this new half-planet. We are working together to bring forth life to this planet. This Earth does not have any life yet. We bring organisms from other places on the planet, and they will multiply.

At that point of interaction with Astrophel, my body was racing, but my heart was so open. I had to experience this to remind me of the veil of separation.

CHADD came up next to me. Telepathically, he reminds me who we are, who we work for, and what we bring to the planet. Unification and Oneness.

CHAPTER 20
Connection With
The Ascended Masters

For those not aware, Ascended Masters are the enlightened beings who have achieved a higher state of being after undergoing a series of spiritual transformations. They are seen as guides and teachers for humanity.

The key Aspects of Ascended Masters: Ascended Masters are said to have attained self-mastery and a high level of spiritual evolution. They guide humanity on its path of spiritual growth and evolution. Ascended Masters are part of the Great White Brotherhood, which also includes Elohim and Archangels.

Ascended Masters are attributed with vast psychic powers of all kinds, such as precognition, postcognition, telepathy, telekinesis, astral-projection, dream walking, and more. Ascended Masters do not conquer via violence

I was meditating, it was just before sunrise, when the day is not the day, and the night is not night. It was stillness and peace, when a face appeared smiling at me, and said:

"We are your Galactic Family engaged in a series of projects related to mass ascension and evolution in the consciousness of your race, and we wish to communicate our ongoing support for the ongoing process.

We are all happy to welcome CHADD and you to the New Earth. It is a very exciting time. We know you are the one who brings peace and love to us all.

Now, we are aware of what is happening, and adjustments are being made. But the resistance to the adjustments is the fear of not knowing what is going on. Virtually all countries in the West are run by a class of elites who hate their own people. From the UK to New Zealand, Australia to Canada, the West is being systematically destroyed from within, and Ireland is no different. The situation in the Emerald Island is terrible. The government has been actively encouraging mass migration by offering opulent benefits to migrants. Housing, food, healthcare, and car maintenance. All paid by the taxpayers, but only to immigrants. The Irish have become second-class citizens in their country, and France is no exception.

For decades, the World Health Organization posed as a medical institution. Imposing lockdown, pushing forced injections, and silencing any voice that questioned. The pandemic is a pandemic, and it was never about health. It was run for total control, with lockdowns and vaccine passports, and medical surveillance. All this is run by the World Health Organization. (WHO) It was not about curing disease; it was about enforcing obedience by unelected technocratic billionaires to dominate the planet, under the excuse of saving it. With clandestine clinics, worldwide organ traffic, condemned doctors, corruption, and dirty money.

Germany and Italy are cracking down on free speech in completely draconian ways, arresting people for daring to state opinions the government doesn't like

The New Earth is where human beings will be awakened, where they will remember who they really are, and leave behind chaos and darkness to replace it with light, love and knowledge. Where humanity will be as it once again, what it might have been like all those millennia ago in the Garden of Eden. A place of peace, joy, and abundance for all. Where beings from which star systems, galaxies, universes, and dimensions will work together to create a space of love and harmony.

The Ascension is drawing closer every day for the light beings that are preparing you for the shift. On an individual level, this frequency shift will help catalyze ascension on the soul level. The fifth chakra will be able to connect with the sixth chakra much more efficiently. This will make it easier to communicate with higher realms. The awakening has, in a way, set off a chain reaction across the galaxy. Earthly beings have been given a chance, a gift from the universe, to make this Earth a paradise again.

For many civilizations throughout the galaxy, keeping an eye on the Earth is a miracle. This is the result of constant hard work. The Earth people have created their own share of ripples in this galaxy. Many didn't take their efforts seriously, but they did it.

Many of these civilizations throughout the galaxy are their ancestors who have been coming home a long time ago. Time travel has been going on for a long time, and these ancestors came from other planets and carried the DNA, memory, and history of your people. It will be as if no time has passed, and they will recognize they lost brothers and sisters, and unite as one race.

Most of the beautiful stars you see at night, many are lighthouses, ships sent by your family to guide you along your journey on planet Earth.

The Ascended Master wants to connect with you. They are Masters of the Ascension and would like to contact you. Ascension to the fifth dimension is not only your destiny, but also your right. You were born on Earth because you have the right genetics required for transformation.

It is God's code in your DNA. A wave is coming; hold your light now. It is necessary in these times of great change. In the final phase of elevation, with the flow of new energies that will consume and go beyond what has been done in this realm.

It has been a long journey, and it is time to let your inner Light shine. This time, it is getting closer to completion. Our purpose is to help each other find our inner light so that we rejoice together in the great discovery of love on the New Earth.

We love you very much.

CHAPTER 21
The Rainbow Color Of Energy And Creation

I entered the center of the creation. It is a feeling of a deep vibration of love there and a return to a knowing, are awakening to the fact that I have already traveled here many times in dreams. It is pure, perfect, and so big and very small at the same time.

I see that Rainbows are to remind us of the color of energy and creation. The color of creation is all the different levels of color beyond the visualization of human beings. As you enter a new spectrum of Light, you can draw parallels with the beauty of a rainbow, where each color means a different vibration frequency. It is a beautiful, eternal rainbow bridge that you are crossing into the next dimension, and it is happening now in your current reality.

As you align yourself with the new spectrum, you may find yourself spreading dimensions, experiencing the fluidity of being. However, this state of flow will not continue indefinitely as the separation of dimensions intensifies. It is therefore imperative that you make a conscious choice about which vibration you wish to maintain; the more seamlessly you will transition into the elevated spectrum of the fourth dimension.

As you ascend into this spectrum of being, you will gradually move from the constraints of nature less into a more refined state known as the Light body. This transformation will culminate when you reach the limit of the fifth-dimensional spectrum. A realm where the density of your physical form changes. You will then no longer be confined to a natural existence of limitations. This important shift will occur at the moment of divine selection. When the Creator assembles the supreme power, releasing the human race from the bonds of darkness.

You will find that the actions surrounding you are not only intense but continuously rise as you travel through the photo zone of the Alcyone star.

Now you cross the rainbow bridge. This heavenly passage is a critical achievement of your transformation, lighting the path ahead to facilitate your ascension. Embrace this process, for it is a sacred journey towards enlightenment and unity with the whole world.

CHAPTER 22
Spiritual WARFARE

Today, in my meditation prayer, I came into the scene of a movement to disconnect people from the higher world.

The Cabal has programmed you to fear. But here we are, all the spells are coming loose. The veil is thin, and the game is over, and the age of idols has come undone. This isn't fame, this isn't mind control in entertainment. It is not some MK-Ultra dreams and some hollow script memory wipe to viral clips.

The people are rising through codes restored, the sleepers are lucid. The grids are imploding. No more lies because you are what they fear the most. You are the signal they swore they had sealed. But your Soul is something they will never yield. Here is the false of the false design. You are not a number. You are a Soul.

You do not know all the developments, all that is involved. Your three-dimensional consciousness is not ready for you to experiment or express yet, but the Five-dimensional consciousness you are in can understand and accept.

People are starting to see the truth come out because it is not hidden anymore. And as many of you accept the Christ consciousness within you, all will be revealed instantly.

You are on the edge of the resurrection of a great event. Indeed, many of your leaders have been suffering. Not the leaders of darkness but of Light. While you have many things changing in your reality, it is crucial to understand that those of you who have awakened are undergoing a spiritual transformation, transforming completely outside the bonds of the third dimension. This shift is not a change of perception or thinking. It is a fundamental shift. Meanwhile, those who have not yet experienced this remain grounded in the three-dimensional existence and familiar pattern, still engaging in the same games, always being at war, and often characterized by greed, war, and chaos. These elements are now acting as catalysts in feeding darkness that permeates the Earth, creating an environment full of conflict and disorder.

For those who have successfully overcome the third-dimension illusion, you find yourself resting safely within the higher frequencies of the fourth dimension.

CHAPTER 23
The Opening Of A Dark Portal
By A Religious Leader

While daydreaming, I went into a scene of destruction and chaos. The Era is changing. Some people in key places took power to abuse it, and it trickles into the soil, or the Earth. They abuse people with their powers. It is awful!

The phone rings, I pick it up to hear CHADD saying, the harsh woman forced me to inhale steroids. It is increasing my heart rate, and I finally found out why I was so confused lately and shaking. You know, it is this woman I refer to as the drill surgeon. I do not feel good at all. She tried again to kill me. I looked for the corticosteroid she forced me to inhale, but I could not access it. She is covering herself and she locked it in her drawer.

Oh! No, I said. Let me calm your heart rate, raise your energy and erase the effect of steroids. She is doing this on purpose because she knows her time is running out now that the draconian leader of the church has died. We are leaving Kali yuga, the dark age, and the age of conflict. We are entering the Satya yuga of truth and honesty. The Era of truth and wisdom, and she knows the era is ending and she will not be able to survive the new energy.

The Draconian Souls group's dark forces are slowly leaving the Earth because too much disclosure is happening. The last draconian dark church leader died, and he was a very dark, negative soul practicing very dark rituals and worshiping false idols, like Kali and making dark masses. Kali is the Hindu goddess of destruction and death. All the draconian forces work with magic and dark spells. Draconian forces work with black magic and dark spells, and the last malevolent action the dark leader of the Roman church did before he passed away was to open a dark portal. He was speaking about the importance of opening the Holy Door in the New Complex Prison in Rome. After that, Hollywood was on fire, and there is no coincidence.

The Arcturian high council has advanced machines and helps these types of souls cleanse their energy and frequency once they pass away.

And they are leaving the Earth now because they cannot stand the new high vibration energy anymore. So, before leaving, they are still attacking the brightest lights.

Another time has come, and humanity is awakening step by step. We see shifts in politics, in religion. With each wave, the energy is coming lighter. It is the ninth wave that is here, followed by a series of smaller waves offering survival by divine intervention.

Suddenly, I heard a brutal click, and the phone went disconnected. This is just after I heard the archon Katherine and her son Paul arrive. Twenty-four hours have passed, and I have not heard from CHADD since.

CHAPTER 24
Gathering Knowledge
And The Emerald Tablet

This happened last night. Something occurred during my sleep. I traveled to a place, and I loved it there. It's my home. There is information there, and there is knowledge that needs to be gathered. I enjoy gathering information. For growth, for connection. It is an expansion of time. An expansion of awareness of time. It allows the soul to move through. I enter the space of time, and many bright colors, like in a circular tunnel. The room is big. I am standing outside the door, looking in. I am expected. They thanked me for coming. There is an agreement, a contract. They are sending me on a mission, but there will always be support and guidance. There is a man who learned a technique many years ago, before I was asked to do this. There is quite a bit of planning. I feel myself lifting out. I can smell perfume. It is familiar.

I see the emerald tablet, which was what you might call tablets, but it is not exactly stone. They were a kind of crystalline formation. A kind of crystalline nano material with information downloadable upon touching the surface with your hand and you will get the knowledge. There were some inscriptions, but for the names of the categories, just like touch here and you will get that type of knowledge.

The Council of Light is delivering a message. "We have always been here. Not as guides but architects. The ten commandments were not commandments. It is a misstatement that there were only ten expression of existence.

"I am the Lord your God, you shall not have false gods before me." Actually was " I am all that is, anything else you can imagine is still me, so there can be no false gods."

Also, the anti-Christ is going to come as someone who has brought peace in the world, when he does reveal himself. And everyone not close to God, who does not know God, will think he is the best man in the world. If you try to deny him and talk about it, they will try to kill you or say How can this person talk like this about this man who brought peace in the world. How can you say this of this wonderful man? And the reason why is that we are going to live under false control. Which is when you accept the mark of the beast. So when they talk about the chip and the cashless society, what it is really about is here are ways they are going to manipulate you.

The enemy will try to knock you down, but they won't succeed, because God is with you.. If you know that God is with you. They will tell you to convince you: hey! I am going to put a tip on you. But this is what is so great about it: if your kid is kidnapped, we will be able to find your kid. Or it's going to stop all robberies.

But what they don't tell you if you don't cooperate with the government and do what it tells you to do, when that chip is activated as your credit card, they can simply turn you off and you cannot even buy anything to eat. It will be you living under control. That is how the devil controls you. It is a manipulated piece and a deception.

Now the illusion is crumbling, the veil is thinning. The puppeteers of false power are stepping down because the real one, you, is stepping up. You who were never meant to bow but to rise. You who know that true crowns are not made of gold but of Light, pure energy. It is about the symbolic end of the outdated system. A world led by hierarchy, ego, and illusion. The all world is fading because a new one is being born. The true monarch of this era looks like you and they move like liberation. You are already chosen, and you are royalty."

CHAPTER 25
They Erased It, It Was Too Real

A revelation suddenly came to me one time, following the death of the Pope. Something I did not relate to because it was used in a different context triggered the light bulb that went off in my head. Where the subconscious was trying to get the message across to civilization. That was at that time of reflection that appeared in my vision this Bishop for the second time.

As far as he knew, nobody had ever looked for it or tried to find the truth. That was at that time of reflection that appeared in my vision the Bishop for the second time.

Before the construction of the monastic establishment where the Bishop was, Archangel Michael appeared to the bishop and instructed him to build a church with a community that had sisters and brothers. Their life revolves around prayer, work, and fraternal life. The Community meets four times a day to recite the liturgical office in the Abbey.

The vision of the Bishop appeared to me when he was preaching during Mass, and he was saying:

"They erased it, because it was too real. It tells you why the angels fell, how giants ruled the Earth and what is coming before the end of time. It is all written inside. It was banned, buried and called dangerous, to now resurfacing because people are waking up. Since there is a misunderstanding because of misinformation or twisted information, the Catholic community has been infiltrated by the dark forces, by the cabal, since Roman times, to keep control over you.

But there are wonderful Christian Catholics. There are still some extraordinary leaders. There are some wonderful Priests, Monks and Nuns, and there are some wonderful, even faithful Laity. They are Christian Catholics believing in the Lord, loving the Lord, and they are magnificent and wonderful. So maybe you have not crossed someone teaching the word of God in depth, but there are. And there are plenty of them. And you need to pray for the Church as a whole. For Christendom, for the Holy Apostolic Church as a whole. Whether it is Catholic, Orthodox, or whatever branch it is. For the Lord Jesus to always remain the head of the Church. No one else.

Now! Pay attention to what I am going to tell you. The Holy Spirit will only work in full force when the person in whom the Holy Spirit is dwelling, when that person loves Jesus-Christ of Nazareth from the heart. That is the only time the Holy Spirit will speak with fire, engulf everything and it is in their path. When that human being, whether he is the Pope, Cardinal, Bishop, Priest, or whoever, a faithful. When that person loves the Lord Jesus from the heart, the Holy Spirit will work in that person. Because the Holy Spirit is the Ambassador of the King of Kings. The Holy Spirit came to teach us and talk about Jesus. His whole mission and work is about Jesus Christ of Nazareth. That is what it is.

If you love the Lord Jesus, the Holy Spirit will work within you. And the Holy Spirit is in you. He will open your heart and your eyes to see the Son Jesus Christ of Nazareth, and when you see the Son through the Son, you will see the Father.

And when you see the Father, then you will begin to love God. When you love God, you have eternal life. Because this is the eternal life that they may know that you are the only true God. So we have eternal life by knowing God and Jesus Christ. You've got to love them. And you get eternal life by knowing God and Jesus Christ. Through the Holy Spirit, we receive eternal Life.

The Holy Spirit gave us the baptism to be born again, not down there but up there. So, are there some beautiful Catholic people? Hundred percent.

Just because one person here and one person there come and do some things against the Lord does not mean the Catholic community is not Holy.

The ultimate solution to be reunited again, we need to go back to the Nicene creed; we need to go back to the fathers' community. Go back and embrace the Church fathers' teachings.

The dilemma of the Church is that we need to focus on the Lord Jesus."

CHAPTER 26
The High Priestess
Mary-Magdalene
Flame Is Rising Again

This is what happened to my friend Joelle, who chose to challenge the abilities of the mind and find out what was possible. Joelle was so eager to get into the scene that she had questions that were not answered in the Bible. She was immediately walking through extraordinary gardens filled with beautiful flowers. There were colorful birds. She saw a Roman-type building and again was eager to go up the steps and enter the building. It was an old, beautiful Church. A group of people were inside, and she heard a voice among them saying.

"Most Churches have lost their way and do not know the importance of the two worlds. Spirituality as opposed to religion."

And that is how Joelle found out the answers to her questions. She says:

"Mary Magdalene is the Holy Grail. She was the womb that carried the Royal lineage. She is the Mother of the Royal bloodline of Jesus Christ. She is the one who unites the opposite. Mary Magdalene was never a sinner; she was a Flame and was the mirror of Christ. She was not his follower, and they tried to erase her by mislabeling her. They rewrote her name in shame so that we forget the truth. But Mary Magdalene was never lost; she was not broken. She was never saved by Yeshua because she walked beside him as an equal Flame.

The one you were told was a prostitute was, in truth, a High Flame Priestess, a keeper of lineage, a scroll of the divine feminine Christ codes.

Mary Magdalene anointed Yeshua before his death, not because she recognized his soul, but because he recognized hers. They came as a pair. Not as teacher and student, but as mirror and mirror. Flame and Flame. Magdalene was the tower, not a place, but a title. A pillar between worlds. A guardian of sacred union and womb resurrection.

After the crucifixion, she did not disappear, but she carried the codes of the Living Grail, fled to Gaule (France), and began anchoring the true Christ path, not through true preaching, but through presence, anointing, and remembrance.

Her flame never went out. It was hidden in bloodlines, and it was protected in scrolls. It was buried in Earth temples and dream corridors, waiting for this exact moment.

And now she is rising again. Not in Church, Not in theology. But in you.

In the woman reclaiming her sacred voice. In the man softening into divine remembrance. In the twin Flames finding each other, not for romance, but for a mission.

Mary Magdalene is not a myth. She is current. When you feel the ache to return home, when you cry for no reason under a full moon, then your heart breaks open in the presence of truth. That's her.

She has been waiting. Not to be praised, but to be remembered. And when enough of you remember, the tower will fully rise.

And you will finally walk again in the truth of what was never lost. The Magdalene Flames Lives. And she is with you."

She also has a message for you:

You have been lied to for thousands of years and kept in the dark by the hidden truth. Every book on the planet is misinformation. Every book in libraries, colleges and universities is misinformation. This misinformation was initiated by the

Draco reptilians as far back as six thousand years ago. The reptilians manipulated all the books to create lies and misinformation. The Reptilians came into control, and they started to be able to control what is going on the face of the planet thousands of years ago. The Dracos Reptilians have different masking technologies to be able to be in a room with you and look like humans. But, usually they are in underground bases in various places on the globe and in a huge area in Antarctica. The southwest region has a large number of underground caverns that are kept extremely warm. Too warm for humans by geothermal heat, but the perfect place for these colonies of reptilians.

But their time is coming to an end. They are losing power and control. Sophia Christ is rising now. The time has come now for you to awaken, see the truth and listen to the whistle blowers. Please awaken now!"

Whistleblowers are not conspiracy theorists. They are the bringers of the Truth, and many have been killed. But the light is winning, and the truth is out.

CHAPTER 27
The Flying Time Machine And A Secret Underground Facility

Quantum is uncorruptible. In dreamtime, sometimes, as the stream of consciousness develops, people become increasingly conscious of the work. Physical Reality comes from Dreams, from Visions and from Imaginations.

This is what I had heard and seen in my dream. Could it be another out-of-body experience?

"Hello, human. Hello people of Earth, over three-thirty-year cycles of human evolution, what happened in the past? what is happening in the present? And what will happen in the future? You must understand where you have come from, what you are experiencing and why, and where you are going.

The abductors are you, human beings from the future. You made the wrong choice in the past and now you can't reproduce and have your DNA changed. So, you are coming back to take what is yours. Now, will you make the right choice? That time depends on you to awaken fast enough.

These years are usually what is commonly used by humanity to change a culture, to change aspects of your civilization from one level to another. These forty-year cycles that humanity transforms in evolves in, so that you can understand the template and map and how your consciousness shifts during these forty-year cycles.

What I would like to tell you today is about some secret underground facilities. The American Leading aerospace corporation's defense has some assets in Nevada, but they have a lot of corporate facilities in California, and there is this shack on the side of a highway in California that looks like some roughly built cabin or a hut warehouse. And when you enter this warehouse, the whole floor of the warehouse is an elevator. This elevator goes hundreds of feet under, and you find yourself under a facility carved out of deep underground rock. They are not reverse-engineering craft from retrieved debris in this facility, and they are training pilots to fly these crafts. The main problem that they have is that in the training program, the pilots experience extreme disorientation due to the warping of space-time by these crafts.

They discovered early on that these are not simply devices with propulsion systems, but they can navigate space very quickly. They can take you from New York to Australia in minutes. They are basically flying time machines.

There is a sign of preparation for discipline and challenge. The struggle you feel today could be growing. You will need the character for the blessing tomorrow. Lean into them with faith. God is producing something good in you. Something lasting that will bring you real peace.

At that point, I felt strongly CHADD entering telepathically in communication with me.

What are you doing... He spoke. Then he looked through my eyes and continued, Did Katherine, named hybrid, archon, voodoo and harsh woman, broke your fingers? Because that is what I have been reminded. It is the second time I have been shown in vision what Katherine, the archon's surrogate and my father's wife, did to you.

What was that for? He knew she did. Are they trying to keep his memory working, after many years of hospitals and mental facilities with horrific treatments. CHADD was in these numerous and various rehabilitation centers and mental facilities, in a revolving door. They were keeping him in a situation of a revolving door of chaos, suffering, and pain, as Baker Acts are money makers for these monsters. And now, by court order, he is kept under Katherine's surveillance, which forces him to ingest twelve different pills per day. It serves them another purpose: they want him to see the archon as a good mother."

CHAPTER 28
The Dark Side Is Very Mad People Are Seeing Beyond The Veil

I was up at night and wondering at... and then it is as though the wondering made me go to sleep and wake up somewhere else. I am here by myself. I am confused; it went so quickly. Then an interesting thing happened: CHADD appeared next to me with a joyful smile. Then I received a Message for you from the Pleiadian High Council.

I have been given information this evening with regard to what is occurring at this point in time. And what I am learning from these different beings is that there are more aware advanced beings that have a more active part in the assimilation of information.

"Jerusalem is now in fire. It is the fall of religion. There is so much chaos now happening with a blackout in Spain, an election in Canada, the rise of Abdullah Hachem and much more.

The dark side is very angry and mad because people see beyond the veil. The ancient grid is returning. It is the energy of God and now you see who you really are, and you see the rabbit hole one more time again. The dark side tries to restore the grid of Babylon. Their next ritual will be the Eurovision Song Contest.

Dark energy can access your house timeline, and they want you to stay in the law frequency again.

The door has been cracked open. The door has been opened, and people have walked through it. The truth is now irreversible and every second they delay; more people are awakening up.

We saw previously that there are three sorts of MedBeds. The three models to heal everything. MedBeds align your body energy, regenerate cells and rebuild what was destroyed. The club knew this, and they kept it very secret.

Almost all hospital procedures are and will be obsolete, and they cannot be stopped. Along the MedBeds, there is a spaceship unit using plasma to replace the hearing frequency in the womb. The emotional trauma will be gone, and the physical damage will reverse. This is not medicine; this is military grade technology coming from the stars. The cabal suppressed it because the healing population does not listen. Disease equals cash flow, and MedBeds equal freedom.

People are quietly awakening a wave of healing now without a medical bed.

The age of surgery, chemo, and endless pills is over. The future is now, the new world is already here, and the future is very beautiful and bright for everybody. For people who have an illness and a disease. The Military has been working with all benevolent beings, trying to help us. They have also been helping to fight these dark beings and the Pleiadians and their soldiers have died alongside yours.

Lasers wars have been happening at night. Mainly, the war was fought in the underground tunnels. Of the fifty thousand miles of tunnels around the world. Expect Galactic very, very soon." We, CHADD and I, are here to brief you.

Expect this to come, expect us to step out of the world and enter another world, because this world is going to come down.

Eighty-five to ninety percent of humanity does not have a clue what is going on and needs our support and guidance we have come to offer.

We are the chosen ones. We survived the treats, poison, endless pills...We are the ones who lead the blinds into the Light. Money will not be a concern anymore. It will be laid on our palms to support the humanitarian mission we are doing.

CHAPTER 29
Tested Strongly By The Dark Side

Another incredible incident that happened was when I was in the optometrist's waiting room. Over at a distance, I am starting to see some people. A woman with short grey hair and blue eyes came to sit next to me. She has a special glow around her, and she whispered without looking at me, "I will be waiting outside. I need to speak to you." So, after my appointment finished, I was excited and here she was waiting for me, and she said:

"The ancient grid is coming back now. The Dark cannot stop what is coming. Step by step, people are opening their eyes and expanding their consciousness. Star seeds feel the deep calling. They want to show up and live their life. Many have special gifts. its their time to rise and hold the path of ascension. They have access to your house timeline and shouldn't watch so much of the negative news. Their brains are being robbed every single day, and they don't know it. World leaders have built a secret and sophisticated network of underground bases to prepare for an extension level. There is a concrete attempt by governments around the world to digitize commerce and currency to control people through money and it has been happening for a long time. It's converting a currency system into a control system where you can surveil, control and influence. Nudging and the control system of punishment and enforcement. Because by controlling money, you can starve people to death and kill them. And the cabal has the technology to enforce the rules they make to control the population.

They are one hundred and sixty thousand infiltrated in every important place. They are all Freemasons managing, controlling and manipulating the entire system all over the world.

Florida Bay Fortress is linked to organ harvest, links to Music Executives. Adrencholide is a modified new type of Biopharmaceutical serum produced from childhood wounds, enhancing brain function, ego delusions, and life expectancy, with NIH funding and infectious disease grants.

COVID-19 (19 stands for AI) MRNA shots have killed more than WWI, WWII and Vietnam combined.

The Adrenochrome Empire: Is what is driving the child trafficking demand?. Child sex, organ harvesting, and Adrenochrome. This is a big deal. Adrenochrome is an Elite drug they have used for many years. 10 times more potent than heroin, with mystical qualities to make you look younger.

Adrenochrome is produced when a child knows he's going to die. His body secretes adrenaline. It is the worst horror movie ever seen. The child is terrorized and screaming, thus increasing the amount of adrenaline that is flowing through their body."

Without another word, she just left.

CHAPTER 30
Threads In A Vast Tapestry

That time, again, I was taken by surprise when I heard a very familiar voice, and it made my heart sing with joy and happiness. Oneness is in my vision. It is my blue flame talking.

"We are Pleiadians, Ancient Travelers from the Pleiades Star Cluster. Guardians of forgotten wisdom and silent architects of a distant world. We are beings of light and harmony with tall and graceful forms, and a radiating skin. Endless memory of the Stars. Pleiadians are watching humanity from afar. Whispering to the hearts of dreamers, guiding those who seek higher truths. Walking between worlds, weaving paths of peace, balance and awakening legends. Among the first to offer humanity the seeds of knowledge, of compassion and unity of Cosmic purpose.

We are not as rulers but quiet mentors, nurturing the forgotten bond between Earth and the

Stars. Our ships glide like whispers through the void. We do not conquer. We do not command.

We are reminding you that you are not alone, but are the threads in a vast luminous tapestry and one day, finding the way home.

Serial genetics makes 12 DNA propellers with the characteristics of every race of Light. You will make copies and thoughtfully implement everything you want. You will time-travel with Merkaba to any part of the universe you want, immediately, in quantum and in a short time.

In the beginning, you will live three hundred years and have it until the possibility of immortality, IF you find your Divine presence "I AM ". You will overcome sickness and degeneration. You will eat very few fruit and vegetables and sleep three hours a day, and thereafter even less. You will go to work, but you will offer your service for free, where you have talent or interest. You will have complete abundance in all your needs. You will live in glass houses in nature, forests, parks and waters, all over nature, crystal clear everywhere. Trees and plants, the waters will sparkle with little diamonds of inner Light. You will be joining the higher realms. You will see angels and beings from ethereal dominions. The highest judge will be your own conscious.

In the New Earth, there will be no disease, no war, division, or contracts with confusion or toxicity. Only harmony and peace will be the regulators of the

New Earth and people will know total happiness as they have evolved. Raising the collective vibrational heat. Stabilizing the New Vibration, that is what all the 144,000 are doing right now. Anchoring the New Frequency to the Dodecahedron's Grid of Christ Light.

We are completing the mystery. It is the time to reveal the truth, and time to see the Light!

It is time for us to recognize our presence amongst you, and time to show you who we really are.

The Galactic Federation is here with you, unlocking your cosmic potential. Activating Starseed DNA and will transform your life, thanking you for your trust and support.

You will travel in space with us. The Galactic Federation is excited to tell you that the dark underground bases of your planet have been overtaken. There are no more dangers. We have seen you go through a long time, and we understand that sometimes you have asked for our help, and we are here today to bring you into the world.

Now it is time to reveal to you who we are, so you can build a harmonious relationship with us and others. Time to show who we are, and the Galactic Federation is not here to hurt you.

We can extend natural lives and perhaps obtain immortality. So don't die, wake up and take control of your consciousness. You can live forever but you have to wake up. If you want that bad enough to do whatever.

So, don't suffer or die, wake up and take control of your consciousness. You can live forever if you wake up. The Galactic Federation is anxious to unveil to you the beautiful spaceship, and the goal is to share with you what has been built and give you the opportunity to forge your own destiny. Hoping you will share the same vision for an intergalactic society and help to rebuild an entire universe.

Ships are equipped with a quantum engine, iDock space station for installation resupply, and revolutionary Trans-Portal docking technology. You have the chance to shape the future of the Galactic Federation galaxy as we all embark on our incredible Journey, discover new worlds and make friends as you progress in your galactic career. You only need to raise your awareness, and we will show you the rest.

Our cutting-edge technologies will teleport you to a galaxy of possibilities and you will be able to explore, advance space societies, discover new stars, and witness the Galactic Federation in action!

The GPS Galaxy Trackers Software will guide you to the right place in your journey. Learn the special coordinates required to transition into doors.

This is a map of the entire universe created by exhaustive calculations. This custom Software gives you the choice to choose safe and beautiful destinations in our galaxy.

Gaia is taken into a Golden Age with more responsibilities, especially for you. Soon you will be able to travel with your desire. As a dear member of the Galactic Federation, you can now travel to planets, civilizations belonging to the Galactic Union. We love you very much, and we are here for you."

CHAPTER 31
Witnessing The Purpose Of The Churches And Cathedrals Built To Play 432Hz...

As I projected myself back to Antiquity. I witnessed, and I found out what the purpose of building the Churches and Cathedrals was, and why there was such a struggle and fight to keep the original stained-glass windows after the Notre Dame in Paris caught in fire in 2019 during the pandemic.

Churches and Cathedrals were built as healing through Light and Sound and vibrations. Not simple places of prayer. Why would they have built such complex buildings just to pray?

The stained-glass windows have been created by Sound. During antiquity, ancestors were already using sound to heal. Like in the Chamber of Oracle in Malta. The Oracle room is a specific chamber with the particularity of producing a powerful acoustic resonance and is famous for amplifying sounds. It is a unique acoustic that can echo through the entire complex. Cymatics scientists have found that the sound at 111 Hz could kill cancer.

By using cyma therapy, the human body's natural rhythms can be tapped into and healed using specific frequencies. Since we are all made up of 70% water, our bodies make for brilliant sound conductors, and many people have found new balance and harmony in their bodies and minds after treatment. 'Cymatics' is the science of visualizing audio frequencies. All experiments are real. Cymatics reveals the profound impact that sound frequencies can have on the human body and mind. And what is strange is that in many Cathedrals, the way it is built, people could lie down on the floor. Benches came years after. There is also the 432 Hz frequency to heal and the instrument to heal.

The 432 Hz instruments incorporated in these Cathedrals were built to play 432 Hz. It is about the secret behind it and the key to healing. It raises positive vibrations and heals.

Today, on the contrary, music is played at 440 Hz. This is why all the Churches and Cathedrals' bells have disappeared.

In April 2019, Notre-Dame de Paris Cathedral, France, suffered a devastating fire took place. But Notre-Dame de Paris Cathedral has always been more than a building. It is viewed as a jolt of hope and an opportunity for spiritual awakening for France. The architecture and art, and especially the rose windows, evoke a sense of beauty and connection to the divine, contributing to the feeling of healing and solace.

Over the centuries, the Cathedral has provided people with solace and relief, and even at times, it provided a place in which to be cured. During the Middle Ages, the Cathedral served as a hospital for the sick affected by plagues. Sometimes housing as many as six hundred.

Numerous miracles took place in the Cathedral with the intervention of Saint Genevieve. She brought back sight to a man and a young lady. As an important figure for Paris, Saint Genevieve is one of the most iconic statues; she is immortalized standing above the entry of Notre-Dame Cathedral holding her symbols. A book for wisdom and a candle for enlightenment, with a halo circling her head and an alms purse at her waist.

The sacristy features a series of stained-glass windows depicting her life. Notre-Dame Cathedral's spire contained relics of Sainte Genevieve. Tragically, these relics are presumed to have been destroyed in the blaze that consumed the spire in April 2019, during the COVID-19 pandemic.

Notre-Dame de Paris has seen sickness, revolution, floods and fire, and she stood steadfast through it all. Continuing to stand as a symbol of hope through this current pandemic, undiminished by her scars and asking that we join together to help, care for and support each other.

Much has changed in the world we live in since one thousand one hundred and twenty-nine, but Notre-Dame Cathedral will always be a symbol of healing and hope.

On that bright and shiny day, I am on my balcony listening to the sound of the waves splashing on the sand. I felt myself living my body and arriving in another time and dimension. Observing myself split, getting out of my body for another adventure of discovery.

I am back during Egyptian time. I am a Priestess. I see a woman and realize it's Katherine. She was at that time already around CHADD. She is jealous. CHADD was royalty and she was jealous. She managed to make CHADD appear dead and she buried him alive. He died by suffocation.

Now, I understand what happened to him when he called me a few days ago. He was having some flashbacks when he died suffocating. It seems lately that he is receiving visions that make him aware of who she is. He had twice the vision when she broke my fingers.

Women are incredible. They are gifted in so many ways. They can do a hundred things at the same time, whereas a man can only do one thing at a time. God created women to be man back backbone, to be his supporter, to be his comforter when he struggles, about to fall, to sustain.

Women realize what God made you to be and what God has chosen you to be. Do not have one change what God has made you. Don't fight with your man; he is too weak, too fragile without you.

CHAPTER 32
The Feminine Energy, The Source of Creative Realizations of the Father's Glory

The vision became more and more realistic and involved presenting clear, logical arguments supported by evidence. Facts, statistics, and other forms of data.

The feminine energy is about embracing your authentic self. Trusting your inner wisdom and expressing yourself in a way that is true to your feminine nature.

It is about authenticity, vulnerability, and connection to self and others rather than being right and revered as a superhero.

The feminine energy is described and associated with wisdom, nurturing, intuitive and life-giving. To reclaim it and your superpowers, begin by exploring how you welcome feminine energy within yourselves and in others.

You have to be your own cave and temple. Women must become their own refuge from the inside out, a place within where your self-extent compassion and where you sharpen empathetic listening on behalf of the whole and not just your needs.

As you evolve yourself open, Love will expand your heart's capacity to welcome discomfort, challenges, and conflict.

It takes a lot of courage to honor your personal values when they differ from those around you, and at the same time speak about it without self-judgment or blame.

The feminine energy is seen as a wellspring of wisdom, compassion, and connection, linked to the idea of an invisible, infinite light, representing a sacred universal energy.

It is not about loneliness or bitterness. It is about the rise, about an individual sacred journey, reclaiming your feminine power, and the confrontation with your own shadow. Not rejected or abandoned, simply reborn and sovereign.

Then, I woke up.

CHAPTER 33
The Great Feminine
Power of "ma-gadala"

I came off the cloud. I had long hair and brown eyes, living in a seaside town. I wanted to live a normal life in my house with archways, facing the ocean and a lot of old banyan trees with my parents. It finds out differently.

A powerful group of self-elected elites on the island had other plans for me. They had discovered I was different from the other people and wanted to use my abilities. I was to live in a large temple on the mountain above town.

I had the gift of seeing the future and they wanted to teach me to direct it. They wanted to control it through me. I also have the gift to sing, but I am not allowed to. Things were happening when I was making sounds and the men on the mountain were afraid of me. The sound is like the wind. Cultural but constant. The sound I make "open doors", and they can see it. They referred it to the unseen world.

It is opening portals.

Wherever I am, they are with me. They are in space. They are doors with encrusted jewel edges and white and colored light in the center. They are opening portals.

The sound creates the doors and opens the doors, when they open up, I can go through. The portals open with a sound, and then I can see through. The doors carry waves, and the waves push open the windows. I can look at what is coming.

The men started testing me. I was put into a room where I was made to perform. They wanted me to change it to help them redirect it. The men want me to make things happen, but for them. I could see everything, and I knew what was coming. I could change it, move it, make it different.

There were three windows inside the doors, and I can see how it can happen in three different ways. The good luck comes; the bad luck has to go somewhere else. They didn't see that. They thought they could take it for themselves and control everyone.

And I started to watch. I saw from the cloud that we live on an elongated island. It is beautiful, and they have tall structures on the top of the mountain, where they rule all the people below. There is no church yet, and no religion. Apparently, we were further back in time before the beginning of organized religion. But power and greed are already present. There seems to be a constant battle between the forces of good and evil.

I entered a deep trance, saw a bright light and realized I was shifting, I was becoming her. The feminine Tree of Life, Mary Magdalene.

For centuries, they said she was a sinner. But some knew the truth. The Cathars of southern France were guardians of Mary Magdalene's wisdom. She carries something sacred. The Church tried to silence it, but there is a prophecy.

Magdalene's wisdom will rise from the ashes, and those who will find it will witness miracles. It was said that her wisdom would return when the world is ready. It's happening now.

A hidden Gospel, sealed for centuries in the Vatican archives, has been recovered inside it, which is the rose grail prayer passed from Jesus to Magdalene. It was protected in secret for nearly 2,000 years, and now it is resurfacing. Those who speak it are experiencing powerful life-shifting. It is a sacred transmission.

Mary Magdalene is a talismanic name and magic within it. A story of such magnitude could melt the entire worldly structures. I am a deep spiraling power portal with multiple names.

Mary Magdalene, Marie Madeleine, Miriam of Magdala, Myryai e Mara, the Magdalene Maria, Our Mother, Mari, Maryam.

It is said that these names are truly a secret and dangerous invocation; they belong on a hidden manuscript of lost incantations and alchemical formulas. It is a lost promise, now remembered.

Yoshua gave his disciples some spiritual names reflecting their essences. The Rock for Peter, The Knife for Judas, and "The Portal" meaning mystic Yoni Gateway for his beloved spiritual partner Marie Madeleine.

Magdalene is a word of great feminine power deriving from the Hebrew name of the ancient mother goddess (ma-gadala) meaning "Great Mother", as the Aramaic magdale and Hebrew Migdal, both meaning "elevated, magnificent, or tower.

In the Semitic languages, mag and dal are the oldest primitive roots, signifying "great, powerful, magical" and "Portal, doorway."

The Latin Maga is a female magician, the feminine version of magus or mage.

The biblical Greek amygdale is from the same roots and means "almond tree." The Primary mother goddess of the Gnostic sacred serpent sects was called Amygdalus, representing the almond tree, the feminine Tree of Life. The first tree to flower in the spring. It is a wakeful tree, the first to wake up from winter's sleep, sprang from the blood of the mother gods. It is also the vulva shaped mandoria, or "magic doorway" portal of the goddess.

In the Inana language, "mug-dalla" means "shining vulva Gateway."

Magdalene's origin means magic doorway of the Great Mother, the primordial goddess, the Tree of the Source of Life. It holds the secrets of a primordial that became encoded as "Mandorla of Mary".

In Christian art, a mandorla is used to signify the glory, divinity, and majesty of Christ or Mary. Even to this day, iconography of Mother Mary is often held within an almond mandorla, a coded work for those who know there is a secret "Mary Mystery" waiting to be revealed.

The symbolism of the Magdala encompasses both the sacred doorway of the women's womb and the mystical womb of consciousness sought by all the great alchemists, shamans, and initiates.

The divine gateway, "The door to the divine," was symbolized by those who followed the Magdalene Mysteries were known as initiates of the Rose Line.

This mandala, or Mystic Rose, also suggested the amygdala region of the brain, the intuitive feminine, the feeling center in all human beings, which is a portal to the cerebellar Cosmic mother consciousness and can initiate profound awakening.

Priestesses used to initiate others into the intuitive, visionary divine love of the Christ Mysteries.

Did I go back to my origin, "The Portal," or did she enter me to give you this information?

CHAPTER 34
Five Thousand Years Of Lies, It All Falls Down And It's The War On Truth

This took place when I was at a Las Vegas conference. A nice woman, about thirty-five years old, came to speak to me. She said her name was Connie and she was from my star family. She began to talk about what first seemed nonsense, but she made me see... Suddenly, I have a vision.

I see a big building. The inside of the building is what few institutions conjure up such images of grandeur, mysticism, and religiosity. It is stunning. Entering the building, I see vast ceilings rain streams of light onto a colorful, marble floor. The interior tickles my senses. The Renaissance and Baroque architecture is rich in colors and bold features, making a lasting impression.

Now it is changing, and I am moving. I am out in space somewhere, where all these patterns keep coming in and out. Designs and waves of motions and colors and lights. Oh! It is beautiful! I am back, taking a huge hallway that gets me to a vault. Oh! I am in the Vatican.

The Vatican's vault has been opened. The seal is destroyed. This was the culmination of a long, ongoing government military operation, seizing the blackmail vault and underground facilities.

A gagged letter shows the Vatican is not only rejecting science.

There is Michelangelo's hidden temple, buried beneath the Medici Church, which reveals some evidence that the Vatican is hunting down a mind that threatens its rule.

The Raphael forbidden painting is filled with hidden anti-church messages. Raphael's painting was not painting, but rebelling.

Beneath Saint Peter's Basilica lies the Vatican Mausoleum, whose bones claimed to belong to Saint Peter were found in a terrible place that destroyed the Christian false story.

I see the Codex Vaticanus, a traditional version of the Bible with changes and handwritten contradictions, and it confirms the worst suspicion.

There is a mummy from two thousand B.C., which connects the church to an Egyptian mystery cult.

Connie says: All collapse now. With the vault open, all collapses and nothing will be the same. The control of the church is breaking down, and you are witnessing it.

They have rewritten God. This cannot be history, but it is a declaration of war on the truth.

They have denied the truth about autism, schizophrenia, and Alzheimer's. Autism is a frequency, not a disorder.

Schizophrenia is not a disease. It is a spiritual gift that is misfiring in a broken world. They are actually tuning into multiple dimensions. They can see and hear real voices. They are wise channels wide open with a shield fragmented. They need support to restore coherence, grounding and shielding

I came out of the vision and Connie was gone.

Wow! Another weird event!

CHAPTER 35
Deliberate Destruction Of The Mitochondria

I received an invitation from Iris to participate in her ranch retreat.

I woke up and had a forty-five-minute drive and entered the ranch. Iris welcomed me and showed me around. We were waiting for the rest of the guests to arrive. Finally, an hour later, we are all seated in a nice room with big windows looking at it enjoying the view outside. A man and a woman introduced themselves and began the lecture we came to hear.

"The Organic Constitution has been reactivated. The Republic rises from the ashes.

The Sandman Project is the Global Reset; it is no longer a theory. The fall has come, and those who see it now will survive. It is the end of the dollar and the beginning of justice. Preparing to retaliate back to gold-backed money. The storm actually happened.

The time of fake medicine is here and coming to an end.

The Quantum Restorative Health Systems (QHRS) executive order has allowed the full development of MedBeds with the military protection. These rooms not only treat physical injuries but also work at the Quantum level. Scalar fields, zero-point resonance, and plasma pulse DNA calibration. Your brain will need to synchronize. Otherwise, the technology does not work.

The pharma empire of the deep state is falling apart right now. Big Pharmaceutical companies are unmasked with their destruction of mitochondria. The truth appears. Mitochondria, that is the main health engine, are deliberately destroyed by Big Pharma. Because treating would destroy the trillion-dollar sickness empire.

NECES quickly became active. The program features wave synchronization, sounds, pineal gland recalibration, and program clearing protocols that can navigate the brainwashing that the deep state created over decades, including TV, school through instilling, and the EMF behavioral cycle.

This is the first step towards recontroling the body and the soul.

The body can heal, eventually, if you have destroyed the program. "

CHAPTER 36
The Healing Wave

It said that with this technology, stage four cancer heals in less than an hour.

When it feels wrong, I always trust my knowing and wait because I always access the answer on time. It always confirms and clarifies. It was definitely making no sense for me, who came to help you.

It is a historic moment, tens of thousands of people are silently activating the Healing Wave without Med Beds.

The Body's Natural Regeneration is back. No technology is needed. A wave of remedies is awakening without a medical bed.

They thought they could stop it or bury it. They tried hard with their demonic arsenal, poison, radiation, and neurological manipulation. They tried, but they failed.

The Healing Wave does not need a Med Bed. It is already working for you. It is reversing symptoms, restoring memories, and reconnecting your soul to your body.

Start now, do not wait. When you feel it, whether with warmth, peace, or the release of past pain, you are silently understanding what others discover.

A new Wave of Healing is returning and it is unstoppable. This time, their most advanced technology was irreversible. No technology is needed.

After weeks of clandestine testing, NECES researchers discovered what sent shockwaves throughout their group. It was a wave of remedies that required no medical beds.

In the NECES control room, the therapy does not stop when the doctor's bed goes off, but it accelerates and does not stop there. With grounding, breathing and emotional balancing, the body begins to create a self-sustaining energy field. The Med Bed is a catalyst. The one who releases the real energy is always the human body. Today, a massive energy wave simulation is happening across the country, silently, in technology-free areas where people are unconsciously imitating these powerful forms of therapy.

We have just set up the introduction for more, as we will answer all your questions.

CHAPTER 37
The HAVANA Syndrome

Mary Magdalene was a gifted visionary teacher and the best-qualified disciple to lead the Jesus movement after his death. After all, she was a Disciple.

"I am sitting on my balcony looking at the sea. I am listening to the sound of the waves splashing on the sand. Having my morning coffee. When I heard a Blip! It was a short video sent to me. The video was showing a woman giving an official speech. She was going to unveil the hidden truth about something very disturbing she was witnessing.

After the usual welcome introduction to the public, she began to feel bad, and she had just the time to ask to be excused and collapsed. She collapsed with no explanation. I was trying to understand, and it did not take me long before receiving the answer. It was a direct energy attack on her.

Well, I learned from watching the video that there have been many diseases throughout history that have created a tremendous amount of fear and stigma. In all these illnesses, fear has been the main motivator. But with the Havana syndrome, the motivation has changed.

The Havana problem is not recognized as a disease by the medical community. It is a time-related and Havana syndrome. The syndrome has primarily affected US government personnel, including diplomats, intelligence officers, and their families, as well as some Canadian officials. Some studies it is said suggest the possibility of directed energy attacks as a potential cause. These symptoms have been linked to incidents reported in Cuba, China and other locations where US diplomats and intelligence personnel are stationed. It is known as an anomaly health incident (AHIs) but a disrupted medical condition. Reports include a sudden onset, associated with perceived localized sound, of chronic symptoms that last for months. Such as disabling problems with balance, dizziness, insomnia, headaches, cognitive difficulties, and sensory disturbances. Havana is not officially recognized as a disease by the medical community. Now, a white glowing silhouette appears, does not talk, but sends me images.

I see money from taxes used to research gender changes for children, and corporations working to keep everyone sick. They are phasing out artificial dyes and chemicals that are tearing away at your expense.

A silent war ended. It is the final collapse of the backup system of the matrix. It did not happen with thunder or smoke but with stillness and the precision of would not submit. The Ancient was cleared, the old memory, older than the first betrayal.

This was the backup system of the matrix and the parasite's ultimate plan. A coded web beneath the skin of the Earth, that was lodged in cerebral anchors and twisted through spinal gates. Woven into the birth line and brainwaves. Waiting for you to forget who you are. It was fed on worthlessness, thrived in the name of healing, mirrored joy while delivering distortion."

The video ends up saying: Released classified file dropped on a journalist's desk: engineered chemtrails are part of a covert military bioweapon program. Weaponized jet fuel is spraying mRNA nanotech, neurotoxins, and heavy metals in the skies over the population, targeting the people.

CHAPTER 38
This Event Took Place While Visiting Central America

I was there, standing in front of something so unusual I could not find my words. Suddenly I saw appearing a young girl from French West Indies appeared. She is around eighteen years old. I don't know her, but it reminds me of an incident I will never forget in Central America.

She looked at me, and I did not like the feeling. I just observed her and tried to understand what was happening. Why was this girl appearing to me? Her name is Patricia. She came to me, and I began to remember. I understood why I felt uneasy looking at her now. I still hear her voice clearly, as if it were at that present moment, when she said to me, "and from now on your energy will drop down, and down... She took me by surprise, and I did not know what to think of it at that time. I was only beginning my journey and was unaware of the danger.

She did the energy entrapment after I told her Mary Magdalene was a gifted visionary teacher and the best-qualified disciple to lead the Jesus movement after his death. After all I said, she was a Disciple and had a balanced Feminine Energy.

It was not until years later, when I was searching for the cause of my low energy hindering my walk, that I received the answer to my problem to walk through a vision.

I was visiting my friend Ron when I had a vision. In the vision was a message for me. He saw a condor with its wings fully extended, and a female voice spoke to.

"VIE, do you remember the young girl named Patricia in Central America? She had freshly arrived with her mother from Guadeloupe when Francine introduced you to her. Alyana and her daughter Patricia met Francine at the market place. Alyana was coming with her daughter Patricia to establish themselves definitively after her divorce. When Patricia spoke these words of your energy, she trapped them. She pulled in your energy and constructed it.

That is why I am here, I came to assist you, said the voice. I am here expanding open little by little for your energy to flow freely again. Patricia trapped your energy between the bones, in the breast area. She blocked at the same time as your heart. Look at your right-hand index finger. It is deformed. It is related to the heart chakra, and I will be working on it also."

Now, I remember when I started having problems walking. My Moroccan friend Gaby, whom I met in Central America, had to give me several sessions of acupuncture.

Incredible! It took all these years to get an answer, and someone from behind the veil to come to help me.

But it did not stop there. The following day, I was guided to look online at an upcoming event the following weekend. I totally forgot about what I found out and did not attend the event the Saturday. Though I received a sort of reminder on Sunday morning. So, I looked at the location and read in detail about an angelic healer. That is where I decided to get ready and I drove a fifty-minute ride to Daytona Beach. First, my navigator changed my direction to drive to Jacksonville when I was 3 minutes from the location. Luckily, I saw it happening and redirected my driving direction. Then my GPS made it difficult for me to find the right parking space. From that moment, I understood that I needed to concentrate and stay calm until I could find the right parking and entrance to the building. I entered the event, and I saw I only had 30 minutes to wait for my healing session and wrote my name on the sheet. And everything was synchronized from that moment.

The Healer was giving a lecture, to which I was invited to go before I could be seen by Patrice. When he asked me what I was here to be healed. I told him, "Ho! I have many..." Patrice did not like it and replied, "This is not what I am doing. This is not in my capacity.' I learned later from some other women that he was tremendously jealous of my healing gift. He went and made a speech on a public radio show and said that he was the only healer in the world with the gift of healing in Quantum. And he continued saying that he has been told that he will be the most famous healer of the century. I thought, Hum! as I remembered his answer to my question about healing in quantum. He did not know how to heal remotely.

CHAPTER 39

It Is Not A Theory But A War
"The Last Battle"

Attending a meeting, I was interviewed. All of a sudden, someone pulled me and pushed me into an elevator and said, I forgot to tell you, Then I heard:

"Use portal 55 and manifest miracle. It is a time of significant change, transformation, and spiritual growth. Let go of the old. Embrace new opportunities and step into a new chapter with freedom and adventure.

The earth is a globe and a hologram, and a matrix. AI is the last battle, but it will not take over. Geoengineering is a weapon of war. The skies are under occupation. The Deep State has militarized the atmosphere to ripple food supply, destroy ecosystems, and wage silent war on humanity, all while gaslighting people with climate change propaganda.

Military and industrial complexes are taking over acid wind streams, releasing neurotoxins into the sky, and releasing aerosols of aluminum, barium, and strontium. You are breathing in war.

Whistleblowers have confirmed that agricultural chemicals have been sprayed to stimulate plant dormancy, which has caused mass death of fruit trees, berries, and wheat. 58% of midwestern crops have disappeared.

It is an agricultural genocide.

Insects are disappearing, bees, butterflies, and pollinators are gone, fisheries collapse from chemical storms, trout, salmon, and herrings are dying in the millions, some independent laboratories have confirmed that nanometal particles each trillion per liter of rainfall, these particles cause neurodegeneration, immune failure, and infertility, and are everywhere. It is population control disguised in the form of weather.

The sky is taken as a weapon to weaken the population, destroy free food and force the world to surrender. What follows is lockdown to climate control, carbon passports and digital food rations, and you will not own anything, seed, soil, or even your lungs.

Save everything, grow your own food, filter water, create off-grid systems, and above all, don't comply. Because if they control the sky, they can control survival, too. And I came back into my body.

CHAPTER 40
Operation MULE: Mocking God And The Divine Feminine

This was held at a hidden retreat by a group of people. They know they are watched by agents who are always attempting to find out how much and what they know. They also know that their phones are trapped. The day before the meeting, while they were settling in with supplies, some suspicious people showed up asking unusual questions.

They designated Lara for this particular mission. So, Lara began by getting strange impressions more than scenes.

Sun shining off a bright object. A shade of lights and shapes. Like the sun was hitting a mirror at an angle and she was looking at it from the side across. She continued for several minutes, seeing various geometric shapes and colors. She sees a window but cannot see through it. It has a very white light inside.

She perceives that the world is colors. There are a lot of colored lights in the world. The colors change and react to the environment. The Light is dark, but it goes to white light.

She enters the conference room now. She is above the group in a meeting.

It is the meeting of the High Council. It is like people are more in spirit than physical. One entity speaking has a deep voice.

They say the Earth is undergoing a transition, a changing transition. The whole idea is to get people to expand a little bit. The change will make it easier for them.

It will be the ones that we can't get to change that are going to be left behind, and it will be horrible. It is the ones that we can't get them to see, and love. It is going to expand into another dimension.

It is like raising. It is going to shift. People are going to go from here to here, and those who can't change will be left over, but they are not going to be aware. That is the whole idea; they will know, but it will be too late for them to change their vibrations. They will die, but they will see it, and they will learn from that. They will live long enough to see what is happening, and let us pray that God will spare them the horrible, traumatic pain.

The other dimension will be like another physical Earth, and there won't be much left in that world.

The High Council knows I am here to listen, and I see them says Lara. The one with the deep voice speaks to me now.

"The ascension process is a spiritual upgrade that defies the old-world order.

The matrix is collapsing. dimension thirteen is now streaming down. It is happening now because the AI matrix is happening now.

These are the codes of God.

We are the High Council helping you; the Sun is also helping you.

The dark side has built a toxic grid around the Earth, and now this grid is collapsing.

Friday the thirteenth was a spiritual message saying that "you are mocking God and mocking the Divine Feminine" because of this code from the dimension thirteen, and it is getting down now.

The High Council guarantees you that there will be no World War III.

Scaring people is the last card of the dark side. It was never about health. It was about a weaponized strike on people. The vaccine has been reclassified as an ACT OF WAR. There will be no more hearings. No more televised cover-ups. This is military justice now.

The term "betrayal of the nation at the military level" is no longer a theory but is being implemented. Confirm biological warfare. It was a synthetic biopolitical attack.

The injections left behind: Discharge due to medical treatment. Neurological trauma reproductive complications combat readiness is reduced anger is exploding. The court is coming.

Operation Mule around the world! It is happening right now.

No more hiding. Army destroys Hollywood's Satanic Empire, seizes thousands of high-level drug bottles, blackmail tape ready to go public.

Military raids have hit key elite strongholds in California, New York, Florida, and offshore islands. Seizing adrenochrome, dismantling trafficking routes, and storming black sites once thought untouchable.

Seize the blackmail vault. Underground facilities were destroyed. This was not an arrest, but an extermination on the battlefield. This is happening while you are writing,

Underground facilities are destroyed. It is an extermination on the battlefield. Special combat units began enforcing indictments.

All land collapsed; biometric torture chambers found; encrypted hard drives and trafficking lists found. CIA-Hollywood command structure is collapsing. Ministry of Defense's linked information confirmed.

More than 200 films have been prepared by the CIA advisers to make boring distortions and resistance common. Streaming series encoded with neurotransmitters to reduce testosterone levels and drive the cultivation of Luciferism among top influencers. Comedians and celebrities funded by money, laundering non-governmental organizations linked to politics, and escape routes were cut off. The tunnel was blown up. Monorail to offshore port deactivated. Confirmed, Getty Museum Courtroom, antique and genetic hybrid torture device found inside.

The court has begun. Those arrested were detained at Guam of a secret facility in Nevada. Of these, two are former Academy Award winners, a daytime host, and a tech mogul with a celebrity wife.

Some Disney executives are involved with children's tourism.

EBS launch is coming and will be revealed. With a full name, crime video, blackmail tape, and traces of torture of children receiving taxpayer money. The army is constantly in control of everything.

The Show is Over. We want you to stay focused on peace, be a kind person in every moment. Try your best.

CHAPTER 41
The Field That Is Higher Than The Mind

I was sitting in the lobby of a hotel when an Exotic and beautiful woman came into my vision with olive skin, black hair, and black eyes, saying:

"Now that you are here, I hope you will listen to my message in full. Before the sun sets and the crickets start chirping, I need you to understand what is at stake.

Dimensions, if you wonder, are existential states in which the waves of the soul experience life There are thirty-six dimensions in the universe.

Planet Earth is designed with seven dimensions connected to the first thirty-six of the Universe. Each dimension, octave frequency, is divided into seven levels. Each level vibrates at a particular frequency, which increases as it ascends, and then we proceed to the next dimension to experience seven more designs.

Between dimensions and dimensions, the frequency increases every time, and the journey we take souls, jumping from one dimension to another, is called "Ascension."

Every time you ascend from one dimension to another, the consciousness expands, and the human body (Molecular Biology) is searched for currently for humanity, a dimensional leap is generated. You jump from the third to the fifth dimension, overlooking the fourth, because you have to go up to this area.

It is currently in a time of transition that serves the planet, individuals, and collective consciousness, your package called the human body.

The planet is the grid that retains the frequency of the third dimension and was deactivated. A new electromagnetic network called solar, or Crystal base (Christian mass), was installed.

In the third dimension, the vibrio of the planet is 7.4 Hz Schumann with the current solar grid.

The planet is receding to the Fifth dimension with a frequency of 51Hz Schumann.

Armageddon (what is called until the year 2026) is the cleansing post negativity restocked and the new beginning.

Change of consciousness, The perception of the Universe is expanding with a greater vibration, because in 3D mode, you only use "analytical brain function" in 5D.

Now, you will be using "consciousness operation". This is the field that is higher than the mind."

CHAPTER 42
My Ancestor Came To Deliver Me A Message

This happened ten days ago. I came home and felt an energy in my living room. The energy that came from the man did not feel bad or dangerous.

I asked him how he got into my living room and who he was. His voice was soft. He said he was one of my ancestors who passed away long ago, before I was born. He was coming to give me some important information on what is happening right now on Earth. And he said, I will appear some other times again when I will need to fill you with more news, or updates, and said:

"I know that you are not aware of these facts. But I came to tell you that there is an underground, at the northern edge of the Area 51 facility, with a humanization program, where human hybrids from Zeta Reticuli were taught how to fit into modern human Earth society. Some prime civilization is allegedly on a planet that orbits the yellow sun Zeta Reticuli 1, about 39 light-years from Earth in a binary star system in which the suns are very similar to Earth's sun.

On November 3, 2020, there was a silent coup and confirmed digital manipulations. The country was taken, not by the military, but by a code of corruption and conspiracy. This was a Cyber war, 2,000 counties, 30 states, and millions of stolen voices.

They thought they were smart and thought you could trust the machine, but now the algorithm is out. Dominion and Smartmatic are not only malfunctioning but are also designed for undermining, with backdoors being built to interfere with real-time voting. This is not a local fraud, but a national one, coordinated and used as a weapon. The media is silent because they are part of it. It is about ending the sovereignty, breaking resistance and establishing a controlled puppet state, but you have one more chance, and it is a nuclear power.

Intelligence already has the information. The court case has solved the grievance. Combined with the ongoing government action already underway, and you get a situation where the Commander-in-Chief returns legally, constitutionally correct with the support of the people.

The Roman Christian Church, for 3 years in two separate trials, five International court judges considered evidence against Ninth Circle Cult members, including the trial's chief defendant, plus the former, and the Queen.

The Chief Prosecutor at the ICLC Court stated. The Roman Church is the world's largest corporation and appears to be in collusion with the mafia, governments, police and courts worldwide. With witnesses confirming the allegation of witnessing incidents of rape and child abuse in satanic ceremonies. In the Neonatal sacrifice ritual of the Satanic Cult of the 9th Ring, including drinking the blood of children.

The research center program, which is a big radio frequency transmitter located in Gakona, was never a research center but a base for mental and global climate. This is not a theory but a war instrument. What appeared of the recent flood in Texas of a natural storm, and many awakened felt a huge, unusual energy coming from heavy clouds. Satellite images revealed swelling spiral-like cloud patterns more characteristic of laboratory stimulation. Some people even heard a weird pitch of sound just before the river of water arrived at an unimaginable speed. The sky opened almost a foot of heavy rain fell in a few hours, and the agricultural land was swallowed up. At the same time, emergency calls were cut down from communication. A decorated army hero died in duty while saving a child. He gave his life to save a mother and her toddler.

Could healing come from harmony? Some Scientists from one of the largest countries in South America discovered that sound frequencies might influence cell behavior with extremely low frequency transmissions. (Ionized sky. Steered aches, migraines, nose bleeds, dizziness, etc. It is happening right now.) While the Beethoven Symphony 5 is said to kill cancer cells. Just with music. Dolphin sound frequency helps treat cerebral paralysis."

In a split second, my visitor vanished, disappearing in front of my eyes.

CHAPTER 43
The Global Blackmail Network Is Collapsing

I decided to use the quick switch method. Felt the signal vibrating in me, I followed it and I am trying to adjust to the frequencies. To adjust my body frequency, but I can't breathe. The air is polluted. All I am seeing now is the confirmation of what we all know now.

We all know, by now, about the takeover of the planet Earth by some parasites. The Elite that controls us, for years, all over the world. They get us sick, make us their slaves and now try to destroy and kill us. They are also referred to as the Deep State.

The war began in cyberspace, and I see that there was an invasion that took place before Israel declared war. It was a defensive attack to destroy the stability of the Deep State at its most vulnerable moment. This is not a spy; this is an infiltration. It is some sent spies who infiltrated the media, the technology, and the defense. They are spying on politicians, judges, and journalists. Creating influence through blackmail to control all branches of power.

This is full subversion. The collapse has arrived.

The invasion is uncovering generations of ineffective leaders. It is breaking trust in intelligence agencies around the world.

There are urgent resignations, assassinations, and disappearances. It is forcing countries to compare decades of blackmail together. The global blackmail network has collapsed, and the silence has been broken, and the files have been exposed.

There is an operation around the world. The army destroys the Hollywood Satanic Empire, seizing thousands of high-level drug bottles, blackmail tapes, ready to be made public.

Global military alliances, and the BRICS countries, took control of the Deep State Globalists who seek power over people. The military raids in Ukraine expose child prostitution tunnels, biological weapons labs, the financing of covert operations, out-of-accounts, and the theft of wealth around the world for generations, while the deep State Network is neutralized in underground military bases and foreign strongholds. QFS is intercepting every financial transaction, sequestrating illegal money and diverting stolen wealth back to citizens. The 250th anniversary military parade in Washington, D.C., to celebrate the resumption of the concept of the original U.S. Constitution coincided with the collapse of the Deep State globalization bloc that had been accomplished by enabling a currency reset of 209 countries' gold-backed currencies, assets. Three days later, control of the Deep State globalists with 2,000 national defense troops on the ground, and full federal power to curb the smuggling in California and Los Angeles, the CIA's fentanyl pipeline pool, human trafficking networks, anti-fascist war rooms, and sensor bunkers of major tech companies.

Military raid key elite strongholds in California, New York, Florida, and offshore islands. They are seizing adrenaline, dismantling trade routes, and raiding secret sites previously thought to be untouchable under direct orders.

The Earth is repairing itself. It is a living thing just like you are, a being, and it is tiring. The Earth is changing, and after there will be no pain, no suffering on the Earth...no more pain for us. Everyone wants the Earth to succeed, but also the people.

CHAPTER 44
The Sacred Triad Of Love, Light, And Truth

That day, CHADD and I are together. I think we are about to take a nap. We are resting in a place that is a sort of cloud. So, I condensed time to when we had completed resting, and it was time to leave that place to move forward.

We are entering a conference room. It is not going to be very nice. They are animals. They might dress well and be neat, but they are not nice people. I just had a flash. I hear the word limitations.

Like "we have to know our limitations", something about our limitations. There is laughter. It seems to be about the release of a new disease that eats human flesh and dies from it. They say it is a possibility.

Is this a warning? Is it a threat?

It reminds me of a few years ago when I warned people to be ready for the time when the

Earth will shift its energy, saying you all have to prepare yourself if you do not want to be left behind. Because with a heavy karma, you would not be able to ascend with the Earth when it shifts its frequency. And it looks like the time has come for friendly, benevolent people from other planets to be sent. The Pleiadians, the Arcturians, and others that have a higher frequency and are healers and are here on the planet to elevate the vibration of the people. When they connect with the father. Because your DNA has been changed, the vibration is changed, and you are shifting with the planet Earth.

But the change cannot happen suddenly, because the Planet is shifting, the body would not be able to support it. It must happen gradually, little at a time. And when it makes these little jumps, people are experiencing physical problems. For some people, it can be heart palpitations, for others it can be abnormal blood pressure, or tiredness, dizziness, muscle aches and pain. All these different things that are happening.

When these symptoms appear and you go to the doctors, they can't find anything wrong. Doctors cannot understand. But your DNA has changed, and the friendly, benevolent ETs have been helping you. You are making it into the thousand years of Peace. The Earth is going to be totally different, and there are going to be many left behind. The sad thing is that a lot of you are trapped in the fake news, pills and drugs that are poisoning your blood and DNA, vaccination shots that changed your DNA, etc., and an illusory world. Taking whistleblowers for conspirators instead of learning from it. You are taking fake news for real because of the cabal. They keep you in fear and false information. They polluted your air with chemtrails, and you refuse to see it. They pollute your water, they put horrible chemicals and pesticides into your food, and even when you get sick, you refuse to listen to the truth. You are in denial and confused.

You can't change your frequency and vibration quickly enough to move with it.

You have to be working on it now, or you will be stuck with the old Earth.

The ones that are deep into negativity will be allowed to live out their lives on the old Earth. But when they die, they will not come back to the new Earth because the new Earth will have no negative effects. They will be kept and sent to another planet that is still experiencing negativity. So, they will be able to work it out.

For some of them, there is no hope, because it has gone too far. For these people, they are to be loaded down with all of this karma from past lives, and they can't get out of it. But those of you who have an idea of what is happening are already taking the first step to move into the new Earth. Because you don't want to be here when the worst happens.

It will be chaos after chaos and confusion. People are changing; they are not going to understand. They will be so confused and frightened. So, the DNA has been changed, the vibration rate is being changed, and your body is shifting with the planet.

There will be a point where nobody will be sick anymore and you will reach the point when you never die.

Many things have to change. like the financial revolution unmasked. The public debt screams the hidden truth of the media. Behind each dollar is a lie, a shake. Every second, the clocks walk; your freedom has been taken away. Your salary is the rent. You do not own your salary; you don't make money, but you serve. You don't live a free life. You are living in a prison.

Fear is one of the main things that will hold you back and go from ascending into the New Earth. And a lot of it is caused by the elite in Power. That is why you are better off not looking at TV, the news, etc. Because the more you hear about war, violence in the world, and all the bad things happening, the disease in the world amplifies it. It is better not to focus on all that. Do not get caught up in the illusion. When the cabal in control keeps the population in fear, then they can control you. You have lowered your vibration then. That has a lot to do with the drug.

CHAPTER 45
There Is A World Under Your Feet

I was briefed by my star sister, Rosalia.

It is not shelters that have been built. But it is civilizations built without you. Train zero-point energy genetically modified food sealed city. Spread across every continent, protected, resourced, and outside the system.

D.U.M.P. cities (Deep underground Military Bases, hidden sanctuaries for the elite orchestrated. 21 trillion dollars are used to excavate the world beneath your feet. The secret refuge is the same elite that masterminded the collapse of the world.

As you suffer, they disappear below, armed, food, and safe.

All funded from your taxes, funds from agencies like HUD and DoD, hidden from everyone and protected by military secrets. As you deal with a lot. Holographic images and Deep fake stacking images have been used to sell falsehoods. Mask face replacement, ear shape changes and eye deformity, fake handshakes, quotes, AI.

You were ridiculed for seeing it and they call you a conspiracy theorist. But you have become a witness to the greatest fraud in U.S. history. It is about power. Foreign policy, fraud. Domestic orders, illegal.

Diplomatic chaos, mass arrests, military courts, every Deep State puppet participating in this illusion is unmasked and already marked.

Nothing can stop what is coming. And now the face of the fake is gone. Mask is out and now the war for truth has begun.

CHAPTER 46
Vision Of Dragon
Demonic Creatures

In my vision, I am allowed in the council chambers.

"What took you so long?" they said. They are all so loving. Now the group is out of the chambers, and they are all here to talk to me. It is about a vision God gave to a woman living in South Asia, in the Western Pacific Ocean.

As Angelica was praying, she saw a Dragon. The Lord, she said, showed her many dragons with the body of a dragon, but the face was of a demon. It looks like a demonic creature.

The dragon was up on the air above the Earth looking down on the Earth looking for a certain thing. As they were in the air, they were going over different houses and then all of a sudden, they came upon these people who had a cell phone in their hands. And the dragons were watching them.

As they were on their phones in their hands watching something, they were also listening to something because they also had earbuds in their ears. And as they were watching and listening, this dragon signaled to the other dragons to go.

So, the woman with the vision watched as these dragon creatures came down, and they came through the back of the cell phone, ending up going through the back of the cell phone, into their eyes. Into the person's eyes that were watching the screen of their cell and took possession of the body.

Then, Angelica saw the very same dragons in the air going into these houses and as they entered these houses, there was a circle around some of the houses. And she heard Jesus saying, "This is the type of protection that I provide." And as the dragons were going into these houses, the houses with protection with the circle around, and the dragons knew they could not invade these houses.

Then the dragons went over Hollywood stars' houses, entered their houses and took possession of all bodies.

CHAPTER 47
The Experience Of The Higher Consciousness

As you are beginning to experience the highest consciousness the planet has ever seen. This is the most exciting time. Light is the winning, and love will go with it.

The Cabal tried to convince you that you have to take a pill for everything. And for these diseases, they created. They want you to have a shot. They do not exist, but it is all a way to promote fear, and if you're afraid enough, they can make you do anything.

You have to start thinking for yourself. You have access to many things on a computer. You have to read these things and make up your mind. Don't believe in what everybody, or such and such person, is telling you. Think for yourself. Do not let fear rule your life. So many got vaccinated out of fear. Because if you are afraid, the fear will hold you back, and you will not be able to go into the New Earth.

And it is happening; your vibrations are increasing. In this other vibration, there is no fear because there is no time. Nothing bad can happen when there is no time. There is no way to hold it back. It takes a 40-year cycle for a generation to begin to move to a New Era. A New Reality. A New Understanding.

There is an underground base with city infrastructure, and a transportation system that has been built. So, an extraordinary number of underground bases and transportation systems. Some are documented as part of the National Security infrastructure. All over the world, from 2021 to 2023, it is estimated that underground you but also in the Ocean, and around the U.S., it is one hundred and seventy, with a transportation network connecting them.

The Earth is shifting, the vibration is changing, and the dark entities will not be able to support the higher vibration.

Henri the Professor and CHADD's Grand-Daddy died a few years ago and went down in an even darker place than before. In a sort of very low level of hell. Katherine, its daughter, the harsh woman who lived many lives doing evil and woodoo things, created a link, and managed to come in contact with her father, the Grand-Daddy. When the

Grand-Daddy was alive, he had the knowledge of the particles and abused their use. The Grand-Daddy and Katherine both worked together against CHADD and VIE. A block has been put on now.

While VIE is now helped by the Star Chamber Group to be healed from all attacks on her physical body, CHADD is taken on an alignment platform for an extended time to be healed and recover from the many layers of his body destruction for years.

CHADD will recover clarity of mind very soon and Katherine will face Karma. Because she will not be able to suck its energy to stay alive.

My guide is telling me there is

- 6 Days is the time for Creation. There are six days of creation by God.
- 6 weeks is the time to correct and heal. It takes six weeks to correct and heal.
- 6 months is the time to complete. It takes six months to complete the correction.

When it happens, it will be God's will and timing, and all will be synchronized.

CHAPTER 48
In True Abundance And The Frequency Of Gratitude

This was given by the Master's Pleiades 12D. We are here to talk to you about abundance, a concept that is often misunderstood on your earthly level.

Wealth is not money. Wealth is not counted by numbers or paper, or coins. But rather, abundance is a state of frequency, a harmonious tone that emanates from your soul when deeply resonating with the truth of it all.

We see abundance as agreement of alignment: flow, intelligent coherence between your being and the realm of source. This harmony is made with gratitude. Gratitude is a creative force, not a reaction. When you feel a true appreciation, you tune your energy field to the frequency of the whole. And that resonates as a whole, and what resonates as a whole attracts more of the same.

Always remember "The Universe does not reflect your needs, but your vibration.

Abundance is not something you pursue, but something you fight for. It is the energy of having already, being already in love.

Do you want more? So, love what is already here. Do you want to accept? Then breathe, open and let. Do you want to expand? Then align yourself with the Joy of giving from the heart, without fear of lack. Feel the change

You are the abundance you seek. The Master of the Pleiades of the 12th Dimension is serving the light, in your Honor.

Right now, everything is available to you. Increase your frequency through simple gratitude, and the world will respond. We walk with you; we amplify these frequencies now in your field.

CHAPTER 49
Divine Feminine And Divine Masculine

This message comes from the High Council.

I was having my breakfast when it arrived. "This message is about the Bell Rock Vortex.

The Sedona Vortex is an up-flow area to facilitate a balance between the masculine and feminine sides. A yin and yang balance. It is a well-known energy vortex site. One of the main vortex sites in Sedona is often associated with higher thinking and problem-solving, radiating its own unique energy. A healing energy power vortex.

Our ship is positioned above the center of a vortex connected to many others that form a sort of semi-circle around it, spreading out. Spreading out across the lower Southwest and to the West of the North American Continent.

But the Sedona vortex brings to the one that we are adding our energy to help balance the energy of transformation. And to make it smoother and easier for you to transform within the vortex. Also, to use the vortex in more positive ways to deal with the magnification and application that happens when you bring into that vortex whatever that is positive or negative of what you are bringing in with you. So that you can let go of all those things that are out of alignment and incorporate more of what is not alignment with who you prefer to be.

A major reversal in ocean circulation is detected in the Southern Ocean. The Earth is cleaning itself and when you work with the Divine feminine, you feel the pain of Mother Gaia.

When Israel attacked Iran, Mother Gaia was crying very hard. A lot, and it was almost unbearable for her. She is ascending and you are going with the flow. And she says, "Come with me, follow my rules. You are a guest here. I love you, and I can still provide for you, but it is time to rise".

It is God. It is the Divine feminine and the Divine masculine. If you sit now on an emotional roller coaster and this includes solar flares, eruptions, and geomagnetic storms, it is all happening at the same time. And now you see the power of the universe. Now, many people are getting humble, and they see that we are just here; we live our lives on Earth as humans together.

This is the plane of God.

- Six days are the time for Creation; there are six days of creation by God.
- Six weeks is the time to correct and heal. It takes six weeks to correct and heal.
- Six months is the time to complete. It takes six months to complete the correction.

God wants you to see the truth. God is flowing through everything. The rivers and the ocean are very real, and so is fake news, and you see that the Earth is not flat.

After years of a communist country buying your farmland, and after the recent case of them being charged with smuggling a dangerous biological agent into your country, your government is finally cracking down. The negative entities will try to make you be the bad guys. But this is about protecting your country, your military, and the simple right of your own citizens to own the land of their country.

Today, your Department of Health just revealed that hospitals were conducting organ procurement even when patients were showing signs of Life.

The Elite might kill you, selling you a supposed miracle cure, the Methylene blue. The same synthetic chemical was first brewed in the 1800s as a textile dye. Pushed by elite influencer puppets as a brain booster and anti-aging.

CHAPTER 50
"Guardians"

I walk up this morning, and I remember one word, "Guardians".

So, I asked my guide what it meant. He said: "You heard The Guardian because it is a connection with the country of India. The Guardians are blocking the influence of the Thugs and the Thugees from now on. Their influence in mental facilities, hospitals, and psychotropic drugs kept

CHADD under their influence.

And now the ancestral lineage of Jesus has been reactivated. Mary Magdalene and the Blessed Mother Mary of Jesus. Also, the course of the power of this mission in this life.

Then my guide said: Elusian Blue (Sacre Bleu), The Royal Blue. A soul identity color.

Sacrebleu, at its core, is an expression of surprise or indignation. It is a French expression meaning Saint Blue. and comes from Saint God.

The new Eve: Mother Mary and Mary Magdalene.

Jesus: Adam

Eve, Mary, and Jesus passed it to Mary Magdalene.

Then, Jesus passed to Mary Magdalene a Sacred Prayer; it was an instruction.

Do, Accomplish, Manifest

A command: Follow and (do)

A mission: A fulfillment to (accomplish)

A Prayer: The extension of the Prayer (manifest)

CHAPTER 51

Another... Dream

I found myself inside a building where you get the knowledge. There are a table and people sitting around the table. They are showing me that everything vibrates in harmony and colors come off of it. It is like I am seeing things from far away. Everything is fluid and it moves. Even though I do not hear it feels almost musical. This is where you go, and you talk.

I move forward to an important day. We are all going into another meeting room. There are a lot of books. A man is walking with me. When he walks, it looks like he is more floating than walking by my side. He is taking me further inside the center. He said that there will be a special room for me and my writings. People come here to do their research and to plan their lives and to gather knowledge about certain things.

I thought it was interesting. Next, I asked the inevitable question, "What is the purpose of our meeting and showing me this?" The man said it is the best way I have found to give you this information and for you to understand and pass it on.

"Historically, the Elite Deep State used flooding to clean up poor areas, fires to clear whistleblower cities. They set fire to and devastated the Pacific Palisades, Paradise, California, and Maui with the plan of seizing land. All these man-made disasters have always involved the same people.

Skies are being sprayed with toxins every day with metals that react with 5G and ELF frequencies, and they are implanting piezoelectric nanometals into the spray. They know that the electromagnetic fields can control your nervous system. They don't just aim at your food and water, but also at your mind. The sky used to be blue; now it is a grey grid of poison curtains.

Foreign Operations within U.S. borders, stimulation of floods and drought, and creating new ecosystems to create major famines and migrations.

The good news is Saint Germain Trust Fund is not a Myth and is unleashed.

For decades, they have lied, mocked and silenced. The Saint Germain fund will fund NESARA and GESARA. It will, at the same time, dismantle the central bank, erase the national debt and annihilate the IRS. Every sovereign system, from clean energy to medical beds, will be driven by it.

No Government can stop this. No bank can control.

The Saint Germain is real, in force, and locked.

CHAPTER 52
Time To Awaken
Your Higher Power

This is Mary Magdalene speaking.

The Sacred feminine exists inside you, regardless of your physical gender. It is a key to a magical heart-connected life, understood for thousands of years, even before the Sumerian civilization.

It is a powerful essence within you that can be harnessed to not only heal your physical body but also to help you manifest beautiful things in your life. The feminine energy is timeless. It exists outside the bounds of linear time, healing feminine energy to flow.

The Divine Feminine collective consciousness has known oppression, slavery, voicelessness, rape, sexual shame, repression of natural gifts, being burned at the stake, and other traumatic experiences that have been stored in her DNA from her ancestors.

As the High Priestess Mary-Magdalene Flame is rising again is the time for you to awaken your higher power and sacred feminine essence. This is part of the Aquarian age.

The world has always been one of dualities: black and white, man and woman, Light and dark. As humans, we are not different.

I am a portal; I am your door to the Divine. I carry a healing energy, ready to awaken and activate the healing wave in your body. For you to return Whole.

I love you.

CHAPTER 53
Targeting Your Bio-Field Aura

That was an awesome travel experience to the human aura.

This is the story of the human aura, which is real and exists. It extends out to six feet or more. It is an actual physical part of your body, but the negative energies want you to think that it does not exist, that it is unreal and a kind of new age fabrication.

They want you to think that it does not exist because they are externally targeting your biofield to gather information and to control and manipulate you. And this is part of you educating yourself on the spiritual aspect of who you are and to better protect yourself.

You are in a spiritual war, and you need to take back your power now.

The biofield aura refers to your energy field that surrounds and interpenetrates the human body. It is often described as a luminous, colored emanation. It is also known as the human field and reflects an individual's physical, emotional, and spiritual state. That is where symptoms are found before it stresses your aura and you become sick.

While invisible to the naked eye for most people, some individuals, like healers and practitioners, are able to perceive it. Very young children see it.

The biofield is a composition of various fields produced by ions, molecules, and cells which make a complex human system with immense electromagnetic capacities. The biofield generated by these charged particles condensed to create a body visible to the eyes, yet has electron clouds which extend into space, interacting with the fields in its environment.

If this sounds true, should you defend your biofield?

CHAPTER 54
How They Do It, But Victory Is Ours

Every time I meditate, I wonder if there is more I have not experienced, heard of, dreamed of, or had in visions. It all seems so incredible. But I just have to remember my initiation with Archangel Michael, it was the very beginning of all that followed.

I had been called and re-initiated to help with my blue flame. Since they hate to see us together and have done all in their power to separate us. They put him in mental hospitals for many, many years, then when they saw he recovered clarity of mind court ordered him to be kept high in psychotropic drugs and given to be cared for by Katherine. Katherine, the archon, living in Paul House, and surrounded by a third dark energy, the nephew.

And that is when the archon's family joined and took turns to warn and harass my family. They are keeping the family informed with fake stories.

To ensure credibility at the time of the reunion with my blue flame, these monsters used the Thuggees in charge of the mental hospital and facilities. They drugged him so much that he became a puppet in their hands and used him as an instrument, making him act like an insane person and destroy his image in their eyes. They handicapped him by severing his Achilles tendons.

But victory is ours. We are the GOD DUO.

CHAPTER 55
The Spiritual Salt They Fear Your Weapon

I thought, "Why me?". I was sitting under a tree. When I opened my eyes, he was standing there in front of me. I asked him who he was. And he said to me, "I have come from very far distances to tell you things you cannot conceive of being."

"So, I said to him, what makes you think I want to hear about these things?" He replied, "Because it is destined to be."

He indicated he could communicate directly with me, by channeling, referring to the same method of inserting symbols directly into my mind. The voice sounded very masculine and very wise.

He said: "The salt they fear most, I am referring to the negative energies. It is a mineral that the Deep State labeled as classified Artifact 776. It is not fluoride, not iodine. It is salt, but not the kind you know.

It is Spiritual Salt. A psychotronic amplifier pulled from crystalline caverns, not mined but extracted and used by mystics, hunted by emperors, and banned by globalists.

Its frequency corresponds to the world's 7.85 heartbeat, known as Shumann resonance. It stimulates your pineal glands like a tuning fork for divine power.

It was buried and banned by the cabal. But the Spiritual salt is now activated.

The Sovereign Spark project has been approved under Space Force. It is for harnessing the scalar energy of salt to bypass the global mind control grid.

Dark budget lab confirmed this mineral transforms the human body into a transmitter for healing, enlightenment and truth.

Some groups of people are putting this mineral into nursing beds, quantum fields, and soul training cells across the country.

Now. you understand why the attacks are escalating. Fake headlines. Cult rituals, psychotronic wars.

They are panicking because soul salt makes you out of control.

It was declared, this mineral is a banned substance type 7, calling it "non-chemical substance". Which means, it destroys the mind of the nest.

People are waking up. Veterans are sleeping again, and the cancer is disappearing.

A business empire is forming again.

This is not a health trend; it is a scalar weapon of war, and it is breaking their spell.

They made every effort to stop this, because this salt has power over 5G, fluoride, EMF cages, Hormone blockers and their drug trap.

It is not only protecting you, but it is unlocking you up.

You are the heir of warriors, mages, and healers, and now the forgotten weapons of the ancients are back in your hands. When this truth spreads, the system will collapse.

And they know it.

This is war. This salt is your weapon."

CHAPTER 56
Divine Feminine, Siphoned, Hid And Suppressed

"**I**t all started when the Babylonian Priesthood and sun worship in cult together with the Roman Empire came together and delivered a plan to control humans by symphonic energy and changing history.

It was never about Christ; it was designed to control, not to set you free.

In 325 AD, the Council of NICAEA replaced the resurrection with the crucifixion. On purpose, they siphoned and hid the true records and suppressed the Divine Feminine. The Divine Mother turned eternal life into fear of hell. They did it on purpose systematically. What was hidden beneath the edifice is not a sanctuary; it is a vault of stolen ascension power, black cube technology that they have used to siphon life force, as well as sealed chambers hiding the true keylontic disc DNA templates of Mother Earth.

But the Matrix is now collapsing, and the eternal life is rising.

You are the living Christ that they tried to erase.

It is time to tell you the truth and reclaim your DNA and return to source.

Thousands of years ago, humanity's memory was rewritten. During the Sumerian Egypt invasions, human DNA was scrambled, unplugged, and the human memory was wiped.

You are multi-dimensional beings, and every dimension is a level of mind. So, there is the physical, the emotional, and the mental mind. About ninety per cent of humanity is stuck in the mental mind.

Ninety per cent of humanity is stuck in the mental mind 3D.

But there are D4, D5, D6, the astral mind, the archetypal mind.

And there is also the DNA strand 10, 11, 12 dimension, which is the Christic mind, the Nirvanic mind. And a lot of these technologies to rapidly start activating your Multi-dimensional mind."

CHAPTER 57
Ending the Cycle of Reincarnation

Robin said this happens to him regularly, and he has to be careful about what he talks about and with whom he shares it.

He came off the cloud, seeing only the color blue, and knowing he was not in a physical place. It is the essence of calmness. There is not up, down, no sense of time or distance. And this is where he is coming from, and all must go through this, he said. One must endure. He wonders how much more is hidden behind the facade, and how much will be allowed to be revealed.

"Reincarnation is not freedom. Reincarnation is the prison system of the false light.

Reincarnation was not part of the original divine design. It began when it was distorted beings fell from the eternal life architecture and installed artificial light grids to harvest Spirit Energy.

These systems fractured your original connection to the service and looped your awareness into repeated lifetimes. Making you forget who you are, lifetime after lifetime.

When you die, you shade and the light is shade, but often this is a trap. False guides, karmic contracts, illusory life reviews. You think that you are returning to God, but you are actually entering an astral holding zone. Mechanisms are built to recycle your Soul's essence back into Earth's reincarnation net.

Remember that you are not a soul. You are a spirit already whole. And you must revoke all false agreements, contracts, or initiations not aligned with the Eternal Source.

Declare: Upon my transition, I return only to the one true source. I bypass all false light and rise beyond all artificial matrices.

This is your exodus, not by death but by remembrance. Reincarnation is not a blessing. It is the forgotten curse of a fallen system.

Your liberation begins the moment you say:

I choose Eternal Spirit, I choose the Source, I do not return here again."

CHAPTER 58
About Receiving

It is amazing to me. I saw myself...looking for...spent quite a bit of time...Then I thought I had perhaps entered a past... But occasionally, my subconscious provided me with something comfortable in order to take the emerging adventure.

Because I have been receiving a great deal of information about the coming shift, and yet it continues to come.

There are no concepts within the human mind to allow us to comprehend all the complexities. There is no way you could understand it all at once. So, I chose to give you small pieces during this time of awakening. And as your mind expands to encompass new ideas and theories, I will continue to give you some more small morsels. By giving you bits and pieces, your mind awakens. This is the only way you will be able to handle the concept of the Earth changing frequency and vibration in order to shift into a new dimension.

It is up to you to make your personal decision on which path you want to follow. The energy is present and becoming stronger. It is physically affecting your bodies. Your own frequency and vibration is being altered. But it is still up to you what you decide, and which Earth you want to gravitate toward, because you have free will.

This begins by watching me expose the murder and drug trafficking place in the largest military base. It is the breeding ground of murder and drug trafficking, said the man that is interviewed.

Now I see scientists. They confirmed they discovered that in the years ahead, humans will live forever. And now I see a National Broadcasting Company transmits a mysterious frequency, eroding the audience's mind to achieve widespread acceptance. A man in a basement is anchoring and embedding symbols in the broadcast. The context incorporates binary sound from the technology already developed. It is inducing transhumanism. The ritual involved swearing a blood oath to amplify the signal, created in 1933 amid psychological operations during the great depression. Intensified in 1990 by another broadcast corporation synced with the cycle of the moon for maximum influence. Linked to a rally meeting, anomalies such as broadcast mistakes that reveal hidden frames with demon images.

CHAPTER 59
Re-activating The Divine Blueprint Of Humanity

Sophianic Mysteries of the celestial rose are awakening now in your innermost sanctums, reactivating the Divine Blueprint of humanity all over the world. They are the Magdalene flames from within that are opening the gates of Re-remembrance as we collectively birth a New Timeline and Golden Age of Love, Divine Sovereignty and Peace for all.

It is the Codes of wisdom and love that have been dancing and coalescing through the ages, with every intention to come alive and take residency within you in this Age of Great Shift. These seeds of light are seeking you, just as you are seeking them.

Mary Magdalene Order of the Rose concept includes a lineage of priestesses, teachings on the "Way of the Rose," and even fictional orders which role-playing contexts. Roses are a symbol of Mary Magdalene and the goddess path.

The rose is an ancient symbol of the goddess, a symbol of the strength and beauty of the feminine.

A symbol of Divine Love. The transformation and the awakening. The mystery of life, death and rebirth.

Wherever you are, religious or not, the story of Mary Magdalene and the rose remind you of the power of love, faith and personal growth.

CHAPTER 60
The Sun King And
A Dystopian Reality

Ancestor King Louis de XIV, the Sun King, decided to join and help VIE as the negative energies keep stealing her money and depriving her of any resources. All in an ultimate gesture to stop the God Duo from completing its mission on Earth.

"It is an honor to help you", he said.

"It is about a totalitarian reality controlled by artificial intelligence. A future where machines will replace the human race, you.

Whether you can accept it or not, you live in a hybrid control matrix, where your perception of reality is meticulously planned, managed, and executed in order to control and steer you in every direction they wish.

And the direction is a post-human world. For this, they first needed to destabilize, to dehumanize and the humanize humanity in every means possible.

The destruction of the family, your children are being indoctrinated by the state, the abortion, the eradication of God, spirituality from education, and life in a megacity.

And the way from nature, toxic food, air and water, social media is replacing real human connection and interaction.

The need for financial crisis and taxation. Endless wars and mass immigration are creating anxiety, depression, drugs, and alcohol. For you to be in constant fear, and moral relativism as the new religion.

Humanity has been influenced and has been forced to move away from all things that give them strength, security, purpose, and meaning. With a weak, immoral, disconnected, ignorant, and unhealthy population, that is an easy target for the next stage.

The creation of an entire generation of androgenous beings.

The final goal is to eradicate humanity as you know it. Once you understand the final destination, it becomes much easier to look back and identify such psychological conditioning, the biological tempering, control grooming, and the educational prepping that you have been subject to for a decade in preparation to accept a post-human future. It takes a lot of physical and psychological abuse to get an intelligent species like yours to agree to its own extension. Most of it, but not all that has consented in the last sixty years, with the design to get you closer to accepting such a dystopian reality."

That was a big comfort when I heard my ancestor joining us in the battlefield. His help and experience will make a big difference.

CHAPTER 61
The Subtropolice Dream

This was my dream.

You are beginning to experience the highest consciousness the planet has ever seen. This is the most exciting time. Light is winning.

There are an underground base and city infrastructure and transportation system that have been built, so an extraordinary number of underground bases and transportation systems. Some are documented as part of the national security infrastructure. In the US and all over the world from 2021 to 2023.

It is estimated that going under you, but also in the ocean around, the US is estimated to have 170, with a transportation network connecting them.

I came off the cloud and was teleported to find myself in a place with a lot of trucks parked, but it is not a sleepy place. I tried to fuel my car at the truck station, but it did not work. There is a brand-new

Pilot PJ fresh park. I look into the back trucks, and it goes through a truck stop. I continue to drive and see that it is a fake road truck. There are police who will not let you park your truck unless you can prove you have business.

I continue to drive, and I realize that I am seeing a subtropolis where nobody hears about it. Nobody talks about this. How can it be I never heard of it?

I am in front of the entrance of a tunnel now. On top of the entrance are flags of all the different countries. It is the entrance of an underground tunnel that goes to all countries. You can go to all the countries inside these caves. It goes on for miles and miles and then it breaks off.

There are some stores inside. Is there anything you need down in these caves?

There are other entrances to go to all countries. It is not the only one. It is secret government caves that drive to any country you want, and they do not want you to know.

CHAPTER 62
The United Field Is Active

It is 3:30 am. I am awakened and guided to call my blue flame. Next thing I know, CHADD and I are in another location, and we are praying before came, a man named Alex said:

"This is not pure imagination. It is classified information given to you, Earth people. The veil is off. The United field is active, and your DNA is in all-out spiritual warfare.

The Mother of the Universe field has flooded the Earth with Divine Light. Every beat, every breath, every cell in your body is reprogrammed.

Your identity is your consciousness, not your body. Your heart chakra is your

Weapon. It is the gate, it is the antenna, and you are the broadcasting device.

This is why the Deep State has been afraid of.

You are awakening. Because your

DNA carries the Universal Code of Command. And they have been hiding this from you for decades.

It is why they poison your air, your food, and your mind. And even more. A Medical whistleblower in the UK said hospitals are allegedly removing organs from living patients labeled "brain dead". This is not medicine; it is institutionalized murder.

They want you in confusion. They know once you access your higher being, once you are fully connected to the single field, you nullify their complete control network.

You were never meant to be a slave but were destined to become a Galactic Commander,

Connected directly to the Source.

They took over your mark, and you will get it back. Your weapons are breathing, vibrating, thinking. It has never been about yoga.

It is a quantum warfare.

The beat of your heart is the pulse of the cosmic law. Your thoughts shape your natural reality.

You design timelines. You do not manifest.

You are the nucleus. You are the storm. You are the Creator.

The uniform field is emerging through the Earth's core, and you can enjoy it, or be buried by it. This is the typing point of DNA.

The wake-up call is here, not coming. And with that, there is a conflict between Divine Law and Deep State Biomacking.

You have to choose now to align with love, truth and fire, or fall with the collapse of the Control matrix.

You have never been alone.

The heart is the door, and the soul is your weapon.

And something is the inevitable law of the universe. What some say, what goes around comes around. The harsh woman's son died after being sick for months with cancer, and the harsh mother lost connection with the grand-daddy, who wrongly used the knowledge he had of the particular. Her energy weakened and she lost memory of dark rituals as CHADD recovered clarity of mind. She will leave Earth just after her nephew, a Computer hacker who passed away from a drug overdose.

CHAPTER 63
QFS Your Name
Is The Key To The Golden Age

Awaking from a Vivid Dream Vision that was received telepathically. It was about four in the morning, and I was sleeping when I kept hearing your name, The Key. It awakened me, and I mentally asked, "The key? My name is the Key. But to what?

And I heard,

"The QFS name verification is live. The QFS check is revealed. Our name is the Key.

The QFS system transforms your true name into the sovereign key to the Golden Era. No IDs. No numbers. No banks, only frequency.

The old system collapsed under its own weight of control and humiliation.

QFS rises, identity becomes vibration. Truth becomes currency, abundance flows through quantum flows through quantum collaboration.

Quantum financial system turns your real name into the key to the golden age. No ID code, no number, no bank, only frequency.

The name is the key. Your name is sacred geometry, the frequency of sovereignty. QFS listens to vibrations.

Access requires no clerk or signature. QFS responds to authenticity. Put your hands on your chest, say your name on purpose. Fraud is impossible. Truth is revealed. Writing your name becomes a ritual. Each letter shines with power. Your energy signature is older than your breath, saying your name is reclaiming your legacy.

Cosmic geometry Passport: each letter in your name is the design of the universe; pronouncing it consciously triggers instant recognition. QFS sees you before you speak. Fraud, ID cards, all collapsed.

With QFS is purity and consistency. QFS can't be fooled. Lies soften the frequency until your name sounds blank. Only the coordination of thoughts, words, and action will unlock the door.

Every time you mention your real name, the key opens, and abundance responds. It is not a competition but a common expansion.

You are the frequency, and your name is the key.

When enough voices mentioned their real names, the echoes would stop, and the gates of the Golden Age would open.

Get ready. Identity becomes currency, abundance flows through quantum collaboration, and it is not a prophecy.

And there is more, it is about the Feminine Archetype I want to remind you".

CHAPTER 64
The Feminine Archetype, The Pandemic Virus, And The Divine Feminine Rebirth

The emergence of the feminine energy that is coming through right now. The Sophia century civilization through and out of this pandemic, and to end up with the world we want, not based on patriarchy, with the dominant culture. But instead, a more open and accepting culture. A more loving, fair, just, and ecological culture.

The Pandemic virus is nothing more than a genetic update and has already decreased and will soon disappear

The human body is built as a vessel of flow that happens on a fundamental level of cells, and in the way in which it produces energy, the microbiome. And so, the bacteria and fungi have to produce an enormous amount of bio-nutrient out of the soil and put that into a plant, and the plant could be consumed by an animal.

And the animal would then carry that energy forward to us, or if you are on a plant-based diet, you are getting it right from the plant source of the microbiome, but you can still not use the plant or animal as fuel. And you have to refer that to your microbiome, which is now going to convert that into smaller parts, bio-available nutrients that the human body can start to manage. And then, it has to travel through the liver and be repackaged in such a way that it can get into the cells through the vascular system. Once it reaches a cell, it is still in the form of glucose and galactose, carbohydrates, or fatty acids. Those are the only fuels the body can use still useless to the human cells.

The only thing that human cells can consume glucose and fatty acids is actually the mitochondria, which are little organelles that are only carried by the mother.

Human beings are literally fueled by a species of microbiology. These three little species of mitochondria that live within us are only inherited through the maternal line. And there is some deep spiritual and physiological importance to that that has never been explored. The male contribution to life, the sperm, has no mitochondria in it. It has no way to produce energy in the sense of a human cell. And so, it functions much more like a bacterium.

Bizarrely, pregnancy is like the first body infection. So when a woman gets this bacteria that inserts a little bit of genetic information into the ovum, and the ovum is filled with mitochondria, three species of these extrovert mitochondria in an ovum, and those mitochondria, a minimum of 200 but probably close to 2000 mitochondria in an ovum, those mitochondria are the most extraordinary energy producers that we have ever encountered. That ovum will then start to divide and initially it looks like a tumor. Every single cell is identical to the previous, just like a cancer cell. When it gets to its 280th cell division, now it looks like a snowball under a microscope, it suddenly changes and looks like it gets a big indentation on one side, and in that moment, differentiation happens. And so, we know at which point human cells reach quorum sensing. Quorum sensing is a hyper intelligence when you get bacteria or fungi, or other organisms, into a big enough community where they start to develop a hyper intelligence due to a larger sense of self-identity due to connectivity and community. So, around 280 human cells become hyper intelligence, and at that moment, hyper intelligence is based on. the realization of unique identities within the whole.

The maternal force here, fueled by a maternally driven energy source of mitochondria, is producing enough communication because the mitochondria not only produce the energy, but they also produce the communication network within the cell.

That baby, now as it comes to the vaginal canal, goes through a second conception. The second adoption is the adoption of the entire microbiome of the moms' vaginal canal. And in this reaches an extraordinary capacity for resilience and immunity within the greater nature.

The child itself does not have any immune system till six months of age and yet at the age of seven, there are ten to the eight viruses in the stool of that child and no sickness. In fact, the higher the virus counts, the healthier the child is. The viruses actually are a genetic transfer mechanism to bring enough genomic information into the child's experience that it knows its self-identity within nature.

So, what we are facing today is not a fear of a pandemic, and we are not being told the truth about viruses, and about HIV... none of these are real phenomena in the sense of a germ. They do not function as bacteria. They are genetic updates to the human body genome, and we know that over 50% of the human DNA, which is a very small amount, only twenty thousand genes, is within the human genome. Which is small compared to a flea that has 30,000 genes? So you are 2/3 as complicated as a flea at the genetic level, but you carry 50% of that DNA as viral information that updated the human genome over the last hundreds of millions of years.

Even before we considered ourselves Homo Sapiens, we were receiving the updates of the virus, and some incredible new data is showing that we can't have pluripotent stem cells without the viral genome within our DNA. We could never be a regenerated being without viral information from a reverse transcriptase RNA, which is the same as HIV; without that, we would not be who we are.

This virus is going around has not increased. In fact, it has decreased the number of respiratory deaths on the planet at that time. It is not being talked about because it is so confusing. How could that virus be updating the human genome such that there would actually be a decline in respiratory death?

Every virus is an opportunity for an update, and when you are getting a cold or a febrile event, you are getting new data. You must then go into deep rest and meditative experience and ask your body why it needs this fever. Ask why you need new data, why you are preparing yourself for the new genetic update.

As for the people passing away, death is a lie. Death is not a fear state. People who are passing away are people who are meant to at that time or have a weak immune system. They were at the end of their journey,

This virus is if it updates your genome, so should we turn it into a multibillion-dollar vaccine program?

Don't some have the wrong science, looking at the equation completely erroneously? Because they are so masculine archetypes? It's just failure, failure of success, and looking at the world that way, forgetting that we are simply vessels of flow.

The body is made of Energy, Water, Light, and Color. The primary thing that mitochondria make is LIGHT ENERGY, and that LIGHT ENERGY from cell to cell is a system of fiber optic cables to funnel hundreds of thousands of fiber optic cables between each cell and at the end of each of these microscopic fibers, there are thousands of tiny little strands

Every little strand is actually a perfect hollow tube that is hundreds of times smaller than a human hair. Perfect molecular tube and at the end is an aperture, just as you would see on the camera lens that lets light in and out. So, we have hundreds of fiber optic cables that can tune the amount of LIGHT that passes from one cell to the next and the LIGHT that is passing is produced by three species of mitochondria that are passed on to the feminine line and then we flow that energy through our bodies and we call this life.

CHAPTER 65
Earth Is A Living Consciousness

It is four forty-five in the morning. I don't want to, but I am called to write this information for you.

Earth is not flat or round like some may think or say. Earth is a living conscious multidimensional being existing in multiple dimensions simultaneously. And it is all happening at the same time, and right at that moment here. Dimensions one through fifteen.

You see, if your consciousness is stationed in dimension one through dimension three, you will see the Earth as a biosphere.

If your consciousness is on dimension four through dimension six, you will see Earth as a carbon crystalline geometric being conscious. In dimensions nine to twelve, pure liquid light and perception create reality.

The reason why most human beings think Earth is flat or round is because literally they have not activated their multidimensional or upper-stranded DNA, and it all has to do with the angular rotation of particle spin and particle pulsation rhythm. This is how we shift dimension and shift our consciousness to be able to see Mother Earth from a higher level of perspective.

Those who see Earth as flat are simply a two-dimensional shadow of her light body.

The higher your frequency is, the more you will see the true form of the Earth. Earth is a living Merkaba. A breathing, pulsing, living, sacred geometric morphogenetic hologram that reflects and mirrors your consciousness level.

Earth is you. Earth is not a shape but a consciousness to be remembered.

The more you awaken, the more her true shape will be revealed to you: A twelve-pointed star, a singing sphere, a living consciousness grid pulsing with the codes of creation.

And she is crying out for you to activate your inner Christos twelve-dimensional self.

You must never look at your body the same way again. Less than one per cent of disease is genetic, and ninety-nine per cent is due to stress, said a very well-known professor.

You did not inherit them; they are responses. Your biology is doing exactly what it has been instructed to do.

When your body is in a full state of alarm, then change the signal, and you will change the response. Because that's how it works.

Didn't I keep saying that your thoughts create? Your thoughts create an internal signal. That signal produces chemicals in your body. The chemicals in your bloodstream now instruct your trillion cells to do something, even if it is bad for you.

CHAPTER 66
The Real Medicine Explained By Foe

For the last 3 days, I could smell some different pleasant fragrances. But last night I was awakened but another smell which would not let me sleep. The dark entities found another way to target me through the frequency of this unpleasant smell. I was not sure at first if it was my imagination or real. I looked out the window, and the sky was pure and clear. No kind of smoke or cloudy chemicals. I opened the door to the hallway and there was no such smell.

Then came the vision to remind me of an event that happened years ago. I saw CHADD putting his hand on the tree, inviting Foe, the spirit of the tree, to come out. And Foe expressed the desire to have the day with us. Foe entered the car and came with us to the building and our office. By the end of the day, we went back to the tree. CHADD placed its hand back on the handprints he left in the morning. Then Foe entered his tree again.

At ten in the morning, the vision finally made sense. I received a message from Foe saying:

"Good day, VIE.

The archives reveal a forgotten truth. The first MedBed did not appear in the twenty-first century, but in 1936. In a secret laboratory, a small group of physicists and biologists began testing the concept of cell regeneration using frequency.

The results were very impressive. Wounds closed in a record time, and inflammation is almost instantly way. The damaged nerves showed signs of restoration previously considered impossible.

But what could have become a medical was instead silenced. The discovery was stamped as classified and handed to the military rather than being shared with the world.

From that moment on, technology was buried, hidden from the public's eyes and preserved only for those in power.

Here is the Real Medicine. When Neurons fire, and the brain rewires, you begin to live something new.

You have to rewire your subconscious code, and you will be shaping your life. Tell others to explore the mystery of their DNA that science can't explain, and to enter a powerful state of heart-brain coherence to awaken their healing functions.

Thoughts act like frequency signals, activating the healing rhythm within the body. Everyone must be free from the hidden programs that made them forget how powerful humans are. They should awaken the deeper technology they were born with.

You are all an energetic Creator.

Some scientists discovered what they call the Mirror Neuron. These neurons live in the neocortex.

The neurons don't act only in real life, but also to movies, video games, and some other forms of entertainment you're consuming every day.

The Mirror Neurons even fire when from actively use your imagination.

Your brain does not care if what you are perceiving is real or not. It responds to the signals to produce real-life effects. And it takes only about seventy-two hours for new neural networks to begin forming.

Your brain is constantly listening. So feed it with good. When you align your heart and brain rhythms with a few minutes of focus breathing, awareness and feeling, then the body is optimized through coherence. You only need three minutes of conscious breathing, feeling and focus to create a shift in the immune system.

Every chemical, every synthetic smell, every processed bite is registered. Maybe not consciously, but on the molecular level. Your body is in a constant state of negotiation.

It does not take hours, but three minutes of clarity, breathing, and coherence, to breathe a new signal in your system to tap into the invisible field that shapes your health and future."

Thank you, Foe. I know many will benefit from it.

CHAPTER 67
QFS, ISO 20022 And
Why Banks Are Struggling

Neil drove his car off the road, sat silently for a moment, remembering all in detail, his eyes flashing by times, then he whispered, "Probably they could not have taken their journeys without…" His eyes flashed again, his attitude changed, then he said:

"I have to show this. I cannot keep this to myself. For decades, the Global financial system has operated with, been manipulated and highly centralized technology.

Every transaction you have ever made, whether through a bank, stock exchange, or bank transfer, has been tracked, controlled and constrained by a system designed to favor the elites. The Elite built their empire on a slow and financial infrastructure because it allows them to control, delay and manipulate transactions.

International Bank transfers take days because they allow them to profit from the delay.

Transactions disappear or get lost in the system because they manipulate the flow of money.

The Government uses blockchain instead of blockchain-based money because blockchain exposes your intelligence.

ISO 20022 is not just a new standard; it is the framework for the future global system.

With the new system, transactions will be instantaneous and transparent. Fraud and hidden fees will be exposed, and the need for central banks will begin to decline.

Banks are struggling, and they know that once the system is fully implemented, they will lose control.

Bitcoin does not conform to ISO 20022. It does not have the structure to integrate into the new financial system. Ethereum is also not compliant. It is too slow, too expensive and too centralized to work with ISO 20022.

When the Global Economy migrates fully to ISO 20022, only complaint assets will be used in the Quantum Financial System. (QFS)". Neil started his car again and left.

CHAPTER 68
The Mirror Hour

It is the ninth hour for the 3 white women to weave the carpet of Life.

I open one eye, and there are three bright and shining lights. I close my eyes. Now I hear as clearly as I would hear the radio. I know I am sleeping and at the same time aware of it. I am sleeping, living my dream all at the same time.

"Embrace your new beginnings, something cosmic is brewing. We are trying to surround you with good people. This mirror hour claims to develop your friendship circle and your life goals.

Even though a part of your life has been altered, halted, or changed, major changes and new beginnings with CHADD are coming, encouraging a focus on your personal growth and new levels of understanding in your relationships.

It is Divine guidance and the closing of one cycle to start a new one, urging you to trust your intuition and embrace spiritual development, urging you to embark on a journey of deeper personal growth and self-improvement. This could involve expanding, exploring your knowledge, or delving into a deeper understanding. Embrace this opportunity and trust that we are guiding you in the right direction.

We are giving you a sign to embrace the messages and guidance that are offered to you. Encouraging you to trust your intuition and follow your inner wisdom. It is a reminder of your strong connection with the Divine realm, that you are never alone on your path, and divine support is always available to you. It is a call to action. Take tangible steps towards your goals and aspirations. We are guiding you toward a more fulfilling and purposeful life.

You are supported, guided, and loved.

The dark entities cannot stop your mission, with a false narrative going around, convincing the people. Any ideology that cannot reproduce on its own must parasitically invade the minds of the next generation, and that is why they have seized education. It is a vampire creed. It has become necessary to eradicate this wake infection from the school. Classrooms are molding your children to disdain, hate, and despise America in its history.

Truth-tellers are silent, threatened and hunted.

The EBS system is not a message; it is now a control, and QFS is a weapon. Every failed transaction, every closed bank, every lost line is not an error. They are executions according to the old-world order. But GESARA is already here.

Deep state is evacuating; global NGOs are shutting down. Over seven thousand sealed indictments have been quietly put forward. GITMO is still active, IMF and WEF officials are testifying under oath, and disappearing from the database. But trust things will turn out."

That's when the vision of 09:09 happened, showing a Divine message. The "mirror date" or "mirror time" marked a period of completion, transition, and new beginnings. Exhibiting the Wisdom, the truth, and the alignment to one's purpose. Bridging the completion, the wisdom, the end of cycles, the new beginnings. But it is also inviting to see endings as a chance to start fresh. A message of encouragement for the best to come.

The Energies portal will open, which will connect the world with powerful cosmic forces. This connection will bring important revelations, and this is an ideal moment to listen to your intuition. Pay attention to your dreams.

The portal will stimulate new energy inside and will help realize and achieve goals on Earth. You may experience major life changes.

Keep your mind calm and open. The energy will be intense, but it will transform you deeply. Trust in the universe and let this energy lift you.

CHAPTER 69
Their Arrogance Was Their Downfall

My body vibration is still in process said Zolima. The wing of the condor is now fully extended. A lot of my energy was trapped, and she is still working on liberating me. My energy was constructed a long time ago, by a young eighteen-year-old woman while visiting Central America. She came from the French West Indies, where she had been taught to do these kinds of malevolent things.

She saw my aura and got jealous.

But Zolima from her dimensional realm saw it and came to my rescue, pulling out and extending my constructed energy wide open. That was the cause of my walking difficulty. My left eye is blurry, my skin and face are scaling, and my left-hand index finger is deformed. My energy was trapped between the bones in the breast area. Leaving me years in difficulty. Though I was never sick and could do my work.

They all got away with it because I stayed silent in this whole situation. But they never got away with anything.

They thought they were getting away with everything. But a case is being built against them. They went around and told my secrets because they are cowards. They thought they would earn points with other people. But that only secluded them from their community. Because a person who's gonna do that to me is going to do that to others, too. They thought they were smart. Smarter than everyone, including myself. They thought they knew what they were doing, and everyone else was asleep at the wheel. That was their downfall, their arrogance. But God is going to humble them right in front of me to see.

CHAPTER 70
Chosen Ones Never Blend In!

Your spirit knows you were never ordinary. While others are being formed, you have been forged.

They got blessings, you got battles. When they got to the platform, you were in despair.

But here is the secret that I want you to know. Your despair was never punishment; it was preparation. Because Chosen ones are put on display. You are put into the fire because those who survive the fire can carry the flame in.

There is a reason the enemy jerks you around with your mind and brain. There is a reason why they betrayed you more than others. Why are you tired yet unbroken?

Christ was never destroyed.

For you were chosen. Not by man, not by evil religion bloodline. Your birthright, but by that God who whispered your name before you were born.

There is a divine code they can't delete. A divine code that is untouchable.

And now it is your turn.

CHAPTER 71
Massive Undertaking And Breaking The Chain

I am traveling. The road beyond the headlights moves foot by foot in absolute darkness. I need air, and I need Light.

The sound echoes through time and space. Within the first few beats of the drum, I was gone. A sign appeared. My spiritual family and the spiritual realms were all around me to guide me. And the universe invited me to take action. Sending me an assignment.

I have been asked by many why the good can't overcome evil for good, though the White Hats are working very hard and doing what they have to do. Your Social Security number is your Prisoner ID. Everything you have been told about freedom and justice is an illusion. From the moment you were born, you were inserted into a corporate system that tuned you into a guarantee, a negotiable asset, a corporate fiction.

In 1666, humanity is declared "lost at sea" property of the crown. Cestui Que Vie Law (London) 1871- The act of 1871: The United States quietly converted into a corporation, under the control of London and the Vatican. Washington, D.C., became a British-owned district.1913 Federal Reserve and Federal Revenue: a coup of banker families. Currency supply is advanced, private taxes are imposed, and debt slavery is institutionalized. 1933 National Bankruptcy: Columbia confiscates gold and places citizens as collateral for loans. Birth certificates are monetized and pledged to creditors. 1944- Bretton Woods Agreement: Dollar becomes global reserve, binding nations to the same debts.1946 Birth Certificates titles: Every born is secretly registered as a property and domicile in financial markets. 1977- Nixon Ends Gold Standard: Trust currency backed only by debt. Humanity is trapped in a paper prison. 2001 September 11: an event tagged to expand wars, surveillance and emergency laws. Each criminal is labeled suspicious. 2008 Global Financila Crisi: Designed to bail out corrupt banks and transfer trillions abroad. 2020 Covid-19 Pandemic: an obedience test, lockdowns, digital passes, and biometric identity preparation for future control.

2023-2025 Implementation of CBDC: Pressure through digital currencies from central banks. Money eliminated. All transactions monitored, A digital prison.

The system was not built overnight. Behind the curtain are the Rothschild central bank dynasty, the Rockfellers' manipulation of oil, medicine and education. The Vatican incorporates canon law into the civil system. City of London Corporation financial command center. Council of Foreign Affairs, Bilderberger, Trilateral Commission, unelected elites plotting policies. Modern faces, Klaus Schwab, Bill Gates, BlackRock, Vanguard.

Your name in capital is not you. Courts under maritime law. Judges are agents of the Bar Association, loyal to Crown corporations. Every fine, taxes and contract drag you further and further into the trap. Since 1933, the US has operated under emergency powers. Each president governs like a CEO of a company.

You are not seen as a soul. You are seen as energy, work and numbers in a system that feeds the elite.

Wars are planned debt. Education creates obedient workers, not thinkers. Medicine keeps you sick to make a profit. Six media corporations fuel illusions. Technology- AI, biometrics, 5G, building the new digital cage.

There is a massive undertaking. This is the most gigantic undertaking the world has ever seen. They have found more and need to make sure they catch them all. Or there will be some more multiplying and resurfacing in the future. They must finish the job.

You have been warned many times that ten days of darkness are coming. The great Revelation! The sun will shine. It refers to the fact that all communications will be down. The mainstream media, internet, phones, etc. Seven "trumpet" blasts are expected (EBS - Emergency Broadcast messages) on your cell phones, alerting you to tune in your TV at that moment. Phones will only work for emergencies, such as 000 (999). You will be informed that the Signal app (with military encryption) will be the only one. You will not be able to withdraw money from ATMs. No internet, no stores will be able to operate.

During this downtime, you are advised to stock food for a period of 3 weeks. Medical supplies, food, water, etc. Electricity. Toilet paper.

But the illusion is falling apart. The (QFS) Quantum Financial System emerges as a replacement. Breaking the chain. I ask you to use your intuition. Bring this to your heart center. True? False?

That was my assignment.

CHAPTER 72
Silent Killer Forces

Some forces in the world resist. We are at the warfare, and mind control power over electromagnetic waves, and some disguised as harmless objects in a battlefield built for assassination. When humanity is the test target, and the atmosphere has become their weapon. With a station hidden in a forest, rooted back to the Air Force and Navy Officials. A secret weapon that confirmed the system's ability to control consciousness, alter emotions, and remotely induce dementia.

Ionospheric, a silent killer of ultra-high frequency spectrum that targets the brainstem, causing cardiac arrest or acute stroke without leaving a forensic trail, "natural" death. Truthteller missing, whistleblower collapse, invisible but real weapon.

Ionospheric disturbances are any of several ionospheric perturbations, resulting from abnormally high ionization/ plasma density, and enhance the disturbance of VLF radio propagation by monitoring the signal strength of a distant VLF transmitter.

The Blue skull carries the Ray of truth and the vibration of compassionate clarity. Thirteen skulls were placed around the world before the fall of Atlantis. When humanity matured enough to honor unity over dominion, these skulls are said to be one of the central frequencies within that circle, bridging the science and spirit.

It is global mind control networks, and organizations that use the same frequency matrix to destroy the population ability and damage the credibility of the opposition: frequencies adapted, distorting the Schumann reflective wave can interfere with the natural rhythm of the brain, causing confusion, anger, or indifference, distorting mass protests, controlled insanity, the digital slave trade goes viral on air.

Field test link to the network. DARPA's mobile phone antenna array, and trap wire surveillance

What started as an exciting time of a meet and greet in an expanding consciousness convention presented as Healing, Truth, and Justice, turned out quite differently. The first day, before the public opening hours, I went around the different rooms at the convention and looked at who was who and what the participants had to introduce to the public. At the entrance of the room, in the left corner, table were two objects that attracted my curiosity. I learned very quickly that it was part of the secret space program. Here was in front of me a man in his mid-forties with a profound and unusual look. Said to be, I learned later, an intergalactic Marine liaison. I briefly had the time to look at the silver and gold objects when I was taken by surprise. The man deposited it in my hand, the Gold one. My physical body reacted immediately. My field had just been scrambled. I left the room rapidly, trying to ground and recover myself. I had no idea what that was or what happened to me. As I was myself in a different vendor's room, I went back to attend my booth and forgot about the experience. The second day I came, and my booth, and one of the two medical intuitive medium and psychic booths, were totally in the dark. We were the only vendors in the dark. I did not think much of it and went to open the window blinds, joined by Vera. Then I went and asked the organizers to give us lights.

By mid-afternoon, a nice man from California with whom I sympathized came to see me, and left briefly, saying he forgot he had something for me. He came back a few minutes later with a small ring box. He opened it and inside was a little gold disc with many other colors. I realised it was from the intergalactic liaison man, and I had to rapidly get rid of it. My heart was racing like crazy, I felt nauseous, and a spirit came attached to it, violently attacking my field and physical body. They were trying to kill me. I had to get rid of the spirit, and I was given the vision of the tools. The silver and gold ones open portals and release many Archons. I saw the galactic liaison man observing me and waving at me. In a loud voice, I rebuked what was scrambling my field and commanded the man in the name of Jesus-Christ to ever, ever try again. The public around him froze, hearing it, and the man disappeared. I never saw him again.

Then I saw a man coming towards me with a t-shirt on which was written "Area 51" and I thought Hum! What is that now? So, I said, "Interesting T-shirt you have here. The man began to explain that he was an Engineer at Area 51 who had worked on different projects. By what he was saying, I understood that he was warning me, telling me what was going on. The man had worked on some projects the government had with some advanced technology, and they had no idea how powerful and dangerous it was, he said.

I saw him taking his head in his hands, as if he was reliving again the scenes. His face changed; the emotion seemed to be overwhelming. I thought he was going to burst into tears, and he said: In one of the experiments conducted, he was called for a technical problem, and luckily, he disconnected it a few minutes before, or it would have destroyed the entire planet. On the second project, he flew a flying object and again was able to abort the experiment. It was going to kill tens of thousands of people. Area 51 is a cover-up operation. Then he said "You have a spark, let me put a golden protection on you, and he shielded me and left.

Around an hour later came a very well-known man for his knowledge and research on the crystal skull with his wife. A Crystal skull explorer, author of a number of books and speaker who worked with his wife. He discovered the Blue Skull, is said to be one of the central frequencies bridging science and spirit. The explorer said his wife passed away through the Gateway of Light, and she speaks to him every day through a dragon skull, the dragon skull he carries with him. His wife, when alive, by looking at the eye of the crystal skull, was able to communicate telepathically with the skull. The dragon skull, he also carries with him everywhere is her, he said. Since she died, he speaks to the Dragons via the Gateway and communicates with her that way every day.

On the third day of the convention, when I arrived, Vera and Pat were already at their booth. At the end of the hallway, there was another conference room. I saw a man sitting on a chair, greeting everyone entering the conference room. The man was wearing a masonic uniform, and I saw mainly women all in long white dresses getting inside.

Vera and Pat were waiting for me to share the incident they witnessed when they came. It was two Black vans were intercepted at the front door just on time. They were told that we were the three of us going to be their victims.

The engineer came back. Leaned on the booth so he could talk to me, not too loud, and spoke. They are all here: MK-Ultra, Central Intelligence, Masson, high-grade Navy... Then I told him: I am leaving this conference, it is too dark for me, I am leaving I have seen enough. He replied: That is why we need you. And I saw him take the exit door very fast and disappear.

I asked only one question from the explorer: Are the Crystal Skulls aligning now? And I heard YES!.

A few days later, CHADD called me and said: Last night Katherine forced me to swallow the usual nine psychotropic pills plus two new drugs. I slept very profoundly until this morning. When I woke up, I found her on the floor. She fell in the middle of the night and could not get up. She had to wait until I was awakened. I had to call the fire department to help. She knows her time is coming. She said not to be surprised if I find her passed away in her bed.

NOONS? The Ninth hour?

Fact or Fiction?

ABOUT THE AUTHOR

VIE Loriot de Rouvray is a visionary and vibrational transformative energy healer, writer and bio-musician at the Bio-Institute of Light and Sound Therapy and has been recognized by Elite Woman Worldwide for dedication, achievement, and leadership in her professional endeavors. She is an honored member of the National Association of Professional Women, an honored member of the Continental Who's Who, an honored member of Worldwide Who's Who, a recognized honored Strathmore's life member, and has won the Hall of Fame for best alternative holistic medicine of Orlando for many years.

VIE is a member of Healing International. VIE was interviewed by Empire Global Radio show Professionals Roundtable and by CUTV News Radio. Her Institute has won the Business Hall of Fame for Metaphysical Treatments and the Holistic Alternative Medicine (CAM), Best Orlando Award for many consecutive years and the inclusion in the Top 100 Registry Recognition for outstanding career achievement.

VIE de Rouvray was born into the French aristocracy on an island called New Caledonia, which is in the South Pacific near Australia and New Zealand. In January 1987, VIE de Rouvray experienced a dramatic shift in consciousness, which resulted in a complete lifestyle change.

Her purpose, which involves communication in the healing arts, was revealed, and gifts from previous incarnations were activated. A visionary and an Aquarius, Ms. de Rouvray heals people metaphysically. She carries an energy that transforms into healing. She has also been guided to write and to create a Bio-music based on a sonic sound with the language of the Light that she speaks for transformation purposes. and she created a New Therapy called Bio-Qi Therapy™.

VIE de Rouvray authored the book 9.1.1. Complete Guide To Natural Healing. The book's purpose is to help achieve perfect health by utilizing holistic therapies, natural methods, and various other remedies. She discusses how medications don't cure the body but unbalance it even more, about vaccinations that contain harmful ingredients to the body, some alter the DNA and lower your immune system, and much more concerning your health that is hidden from the public.

Then VIE de Rouvray also authored her first volume, "Beware of the Almighty; The Destiny of the doG", a theory thriller about the journey of a tainted angel and about the culmination of historical events that will interact with the prophecies of the future days. The book features the ancient city of Antioch, fallen angels, ancient legends, and a secret sect created in the days of Jesus. The book illustrated a modern adventure through which Christianity is introduced to the world.

VIE de Rouvray's second book is titled "Time is Ticking; The Fifth Amendment." It explains the world today and illustrates another fascinating and historical adventure that includes the return of Jesus and Mary Magdalene, who demonstrate the path of Divine love.

VIE de Rouvray wrote her third volume, "Karma through the Window of Time.". It is about two angels at work. One is a physical Light and vibration healer guided to be reconnected to her original essence that is now here in a different life to see the transformation from the age of Pisces to the age of Aquarius.

Then she wrote the 4th, 5th, 6th Books of the series "New Century, New Era, New Experiences", "Intonex; The Secret Harmony of Life", "The Genome of the Ancient Creators" and "The Phoenix with the Crystal Plumage" and "The Great Awakening."

VIE Loriot de Rouvray speaks the language of the Light that is the galactic language of Love and Light. She tones, chants, and hand signs the language of the Light that is instant communication with the infinite mind using pictographic cybernetics. It is the parent language of the deity used overall plan to design to outline a procedure, to code knowledge into Crystal, etc., to reach many planetary worlds and realities simultaneously, and fuse the different languages into the same scenario. The universal language is light-coded information to reawaken the DNA and dormant aspect of your divine blueprint. It carries encodements for frequency healing, activating the DNA. It is used for healing issues, for toning, meditating, and aligning. Light language, in short, is a carrier of codes and vibrational frequencies of the fifth dimension, vibrating high enough to be able to channel Light language.

She believes that spiritual growth, vitality, and wellness are the link to humans' primary purpose. In her eyes, life is a game, an adventure that has to be experienced, examined, and understood in order to restore balance in body, mind, and spirit. Ms. de Rouvray believes the end result of infinite growth is to realize Oneness, and thus the meaning of life is growth in consciousness through mental, physical, and mind experiences, like pain, stress, anger, fear, illnesses, and diseases. She says that her purpose and intentions are a visionary healer, vibrational transformative energy practitioner, spiritual and metaphysical teacher, and an Aquarius. She helps teach the body to heal at a deep cellular level, and it is designed to assist people in opening their own self-healing ability and personal empowerment. She uses, when needed, Sacred Geometry because it transmits energy and awareness for soul awakening. Many frequencies of energy are very different in their qualities.

ABOUT HEALER VIE

Her name is VIE; it means life. Life, because it transforms. Which enables her to reconnect you to the source, and be whole again, to self-heal.

This is an approach beyond conventional therapies for everyone interested in the alternative and holistic field. Wellness and Health were never about chemical drugs, but about frequency and vibrational energy,

By tuning your frequency, you will access your higher expression and type into the unified field of creation to heal. This is an advanced, energetic, transformative therapy treatment, balancing the body at the cellular level, the root cause. This is a frequency-based Light Language Sound vibration that transforms, and the person in treatment is guided and able to witness the change happening, seeing it.

This is a unique opportunity given to you. Not everyone carries this transformative vibrational energy and works directly under the Divine to reconnect you to the Source to self-heal and ascend to the Fifth dimension.

VIE healing and calibrating sessions are Worldwide and nationally remote. (Distant mode). https://healervie.com/

She owns the Institute of Biostimulation of Light and Sound Therapy. The Creator of a new therapy called Bio-Qi Therapy™.

Email: instituteofbiostimulation@yahoo.com

Website: www.instituteoflightandsound.com

Website: naturalhealingorlando.com/bio-qi/therapy

Website: https://authorvie.com

Website: https://healervie.com

Twitter: www.twitter.com/Lightsound4

facebook:www.facebook.com/BioinstituteOfLights AndSound

YouTube channel: Institute of Light and Sound Leaping Horizon series.